# Nursery in Bloom

## HEATHER MORRIS

# ACKNOWLEDGMENTS

A great big thank you goes out to Holly Singer for creating and painting the cover! She took my ideas and created the perfect image!

1

"Leah! Where are you?" I hear my husband yell at me from downstairs.

"Upstairs, why?" I yell back and start towards the stairs so I can meet him at the top. I'm almost eight months pregnant and know better than to fly down the stairs to meet him eye to eye.

Looking down at Lewis I can clearly see that he's had too much to drink. Again. They must've lost the game today because that's when he normally gets this way. He's a pitcher for the New York Yankees so I can only imagine why he's three sheets to the wind.

"What are you doing up there?" he slurs out a little too loud. His voice echoes through the whole house. The marble floors don't help the sound carrying.

"I was putting baby clothes away. I take it you guys lost?" I say to him as he starts to come up the stairs.

"Why would you ask me such a thing? You're an ungrateful bitch! You don't care what I go through every day to bring you this nice house and nice clothes." Almost to the top, he misses a step and grabs ahold of the banister. I leap forward to help him afraid to see him fall down the stairs. It's a long way down and that would be terrible.

As I help him make it to the top of the stairs, he jerks his arm out of my grasp and starts yelling again.

"Don't touch me you whore. You are nothing but a whore who sleeps with all of my teammates. You don't know how to be a good wife. You spend all my money and leave me with nothing."

"Lewis you don't know what you're talking about. You are just drunk. Let's get you to bed and you'll feel better in the morning." I shake my head and sigh knowing this happens all too often anymore.

Lewis drinks and drinks until he can't take anymore then I have to deal with his outrageous claims. None of it is true; I am nothing but a faithful, devoted wife that is also the mother of his child growing inside me. Where he gets this stuff from is beyond me. It's always the same thing when he's like this. He got hurt last season and hasn't been released yet this season to play, leaving him angry and vulnerable. Lewis in this state and alcohol isn't a good combination. Sometimes he tries to get physical and violent but I have always been lucky enough to keep away from his flying fists. I have had to call a contractor many times to fix holes in the walls and broken doors. Better them than me I guess.

I reach over and wrap my arm around his waist hoping he will let me get him to bed before anything else happens tonight. He swings both fists and connects with both sides of my face. Pain beyond anything I have ever experienced rushes through me. He continues to hit and connect no matter where I move my head. I let go of him and try to grab his arms. But as I do, he realizes and shoves me with all his might, he catches me off guard and off balance.

Before I know it I am the one falling backwards towards the stairs. And then I feel myself falling back and down. I try to grab the banister but can't get it before beginning to fall backwards and feel my feet go over my head and I hit my stomach on the hard stairs once, then twice, then a third time. Pain is shooting through my whole body but all I can think about is the baby.

Once I quit falling, I vaguely hear Lewis laughing. It's very faint and I'm not real sure if I imagined it or not. I try to open my eyes but they're swelling shut from the trauma and his fists. My abdomen is throbbing with pain and I try to move my hands up to massage it but I can't seem to find the strength to do so. I'm afraid both arms are broken and can't move my legs. Am I dead? My baby…

I hear a soft voice crying and saying my name and once again I try to open my eyes. I know the voice is my housekeeper and she must have seen the whole thing. Is Lewis coming down the stairs to help? Did he mean to do this?

"Miss Leah, oh my goodness! I called 911 and they're on their way. Can you hear me Miss Leah?"

I groan out what I can and she says again, "Help is on the way Miss Leah. I called your dad too."

"Lewis." I groan out again wondering where he is. Is he sitting by me? Where is he?

"He isn't here Miss Leah." I can feel her stroke my cheek and right my clothing. She is so thoughtful to not want my lady parts showing when the medics arrive. Little do we all know, that is the least of my problems. I have just fallen down a tall flight of marble stairs. Pregnant.

I hear sirens becoming louder and louder. Help is here. Please tell me they can help my baby. My stomach hurts so terribly that I'm not sure I can wait much longer. I have never hurt this bad in my entire life. I hope they can help Shan… And out I go.

2

"Where's my daughter? Leah Frankle! Where is she?" I hear my dad's booming voice come breaking through my haze. I hear him but where is he? Where am I?

"Dad? Where are you?" I croak out, not sure if anyone can hear me.

"He's just outside ma'am. I'll get him for you." Why isn't he in here with me?

"Leah, I'm here. You scared me so much. I'm so sorry this happened to you. Please tell me you're going to be okay."

"Dad? How's the baby? How's Shannon? Is she okay Dad?"

"Leah, baby, you need to get stronger before we worry about anything else. They did a C-section and your body is stapled together. You have broken bones and two fractured ankles. Your left wrist is sprained and you have a severe concussion. Please stay still and rest. I can't lose you."

The sound of Dad's voice scares me. Something is wrong. I had Shannon, so what's wrong? I don't care what's wrong with me; I just want to know Shannon is okay.

"Dad, she's my child. I want to know how she is. Please tell me she's okay." He grabs my hand and I plead to him over this.

"Leah, she didn't make it. The trauma she received during the fall was too much for her. I'm so sorry."

"Dad no! She can't be dead. Dad!!!" I scream and try to sit up but am stopped from the excruciating pain shooting all over my body. He wraps his arms around me and pats my back as I lose control.

How could this have happened? How can my baby be gone? She was supposed to be born in two months and I was going to have a beautiful little girl. This morning I woke up full of hope and promise with a baby girl coming and now I'm alone. And empty. I really am empty, she isn't growing inside me anymore. I can't keep the tears at bay now. Dad holds me while I cry and mourn my little girl and the life we were going to have. I'm completely heartbroken.

\*\*\*\*\*\*\*\*\*\*\*\*\*\*\*\*\*\*

"Hey sweetheart. How ya feeling today?"

"Hi Dad. Good as can be I guess."

"Are you up for company? Lewis is in the waiting room and wants to talk to you."

"No Dad. I don't want to see him or hear a word he has to say. He did this."

"Okay, I'll talk to him outside. You rest. I won't let him near you."

"Thanks Dad." I roll over in my hospital bed and look out the window. With clouds looking like cotton candy in the sky I envision Shannon being up there in Heaven with my Mom. That thought makes it a little easier to know neither of them is here now.

"Take care of her for me Mama." Tears stream down my cheeks as my heart continues to break.

After a half hour or so Dad comes back in the room looking a bit off. I can only imagine what was said between those two. After what Lewis did my father will never let him get away with it. I wonder if he called the cops? I don't want to deal with any of that or the media. The media, ugh.

"Dad, what's with that look on your face?"

"You have nothing to worry about Leah. Lewis is going to grant a quick divorce and a very large settlement. He will never come near you again. Ever again. He realizes what he did and I think he is very upset too but knows it's all his fault. He's going to check into rehab and sell the house. While he's gone we'll get all your stuff out of that house and get you moved into my house for now."

"Wow. This is all so much Dad. Thank you for taking charge while I couldn't even think of what to do. It's just too much!" Crying again Dad wraps me in his arms and kisses the top of my head. I feel broken and this man is the only thing I have left. The only thing.

Two weeks later I'm looking for another place to live because living with my father is not fun. He is fawning over me like a child. He never treated me like this when I was a child. Ugh. I know he means the best but he's driving me nuts!

We had Shannon's little graveside service a few days after I got out of the hospital and Lewis was unable to come because of rehab and the deal he made with Dad. It was very very sad but I know she is in good hands with Mama. I have had a little bit of time to get over it the best I can. I will always remember the dreams I had for her but things happen for a reason and I can just pray that I know what those reasons are someday soon.

I have to hobble around on crutches because of the two walking casts I have and my one wrist still has a cast on it from the sprain which I had to have surgery on. My face is still black and blue so I don't really go out in public yet. I look horrible and would have to explain to the world what happened to me. And with Lewis being in rehab now they would put the pieces together. I haven't been to work since before I started showing and have since then terminated my contract with Chanel because being in public in front of the cameras is something I'm not sure I want to ever do again.

The divorce was finalized last week too so I'm not married to Lewis anymore. That sounds so strange to say. Within a few weeks' time my life has been turned upside down. I lost my husband and child in such a quick moment. He has been to rehab and sounds like he is doing better from what Dad tells me. I can't help but to feel sorry for him but then again I am very mad at him too for what he did. His life was spiraling out of control and seemed to take mine with it. No more. He will never affect my life again.

*******************

"Leah, I need to talk to you. Do you have a minute?"

"Sure Dad, what's up?"

"I just got a call from Colvin. Grandpa Stampley has passed away."

"Oh my goodness Dad! Are you okay?"

"Yes, I feel bad for not being there. Do you think you would want to go for the funeral?"

"Not like this Dad. I would be looking over my shoulder. You go though."

"I can't leave you Leah. Grandpa would understand."

"No Dad. You go, I will be fine."

"Are you sure?"

"Go Dad. He was your father."

"Okay I will. Can you have your old housekeeper come help you here while I'm gone?"

"I'll call her right now. Go make your trip plans Dad. I'll be fine."

Wow now Grandpa Stampley is gone. I feel so terrible that I can't go to say good-bye. He was such a wonderful and kind man. Poor Dad. What more could happen?

It's been a week since Dad got back from Colvin, Oklahoma where he grew up. He said the funeral was a great tribute to the man Grandpa was. He has been trying to figure out what Grandpa wanted done with Stampley's which is the nursery that he owned. And their house. The house Dad grew up in. Dad has been awaiting a call from Roger Yasser, Grandpa's attorney.

I'm standing in the kitchen making lunch when the phone rings so I reach over and put it on speaker.

"Hello?"

"Is Leah available please?"

"Speaking. What can I do for you?"

"This is Roger Yasser, I am your Grandfather's attorney here in Colvin, Oklahoma."

"Oh yes, Dad has been awaiting your call. Let me go get him."

"No, that's not necessary, I called to talk to you ma'am."

"Me? What would you need to talk to me about?"

"I need you to be in my office tomorrow at 2 pm for the reading of your Grandpa's will."

"Me? What about my Dad?"

"Just you, Mrs. Frankle, can you be here?"

"That's tomorrow. I have to come all the way there? You can't just tell me over the phone?"

"No ma'am. Do you think you can make it?"

"I suppose if that's the only way. I'll be there."

"Thank you Leah and I look forward to meeting you. Take care."

"Thank you." Now that was very strange. What in the world would I need to be there and not Dad?

"Dad? I just got a call from Grandpa's attorney."

"Ya, he said he was going to call you. Are you going?"

"How long have you known?"

"Since this morning when he called me. Grandpa had special instructions for you and only you."

"This is bizarre Dad. Why wouldn't you need to be there? Why me?"

"You were his only grandchild Leah."

"You were his only child though Dad."

"He had a letter for me that was left for me. Roger gave it to me when I was there."

"What about the house and the nursery?"

"I don't know Leah. We will figure that out as we go along. You need to go to Colvin and see what he has to say to you."

"Must be a lot if I have to fly there on such short notice."

"I'll make the flight arrangements for you Leah."

"Alright. Lunch will be ready in a bit."

Dad's taking this very well but I'm still confused. What in the world is going on? Why would I need to be in Oklahoma just to receive a letter Grandpa left me? I guess I'll soon find out.

*******************

"Austin, this is Roger Yasser. I need you to come to my office today at 2pm. I have some information for you regarding Jack Stampley's nursery. Once again, 2pm, my office. Thanks." I hear on my voicemail after coming in from helping Aiden with a new horse.

What in the world would an attorney want with me and Jack? I look at my watch and notice its 1:00 pm. I will know that answer soon enough. Just enough time to clean up and head into town.

As I pull up in front of Roger's office I get a strange feeling that things are going to get a little crazy in there. The hair is standing up on the back of my neck.

"No time like the present to figure out why." I say as I get out of my pickup and head inside the office.

"He is waiting in his office Austin. Go right on in." Penny Lancaster says as I step inside. She has worked in this office since before Roger's father retired. In this small town everyone knows everyone.

Except for the red head sitting in the office with Roger. This is strange. She is gorgeous though. Long hair to the middle of her back and curls, my goodness. They look so soft. I ache to touch one between my fingers but rein in my thoughts. How could one woman I have never met before stir so many thoughts inside me in a split second? And why do I need to be in here with someone I have never met to talk about Stampley's? This is not going to be good if she is from one of those big corporations that have been pressuring the citizens of Colvin to sell so they could build big box stores.

Roger must have read my thoughts because he quickly says, "Thank you for coming Austin. This is Leah Frankle. I'm not sure if you have met, she's Jack Stampley's granddaughter. She's here just like you to hear the reading of Jack's will."

This is Jack's granddaughter? Reality hits me like a Mac truck! I used to have the biggest crush on her when she would come spend the summers with Jack and hang out around Stampley's. I have worked with Jack at Stampley's since I was old enough to go there with my mom. Once I was old enough to work, Jack gave me a job. I always looked forward to the summers when Leah would come until she was in high school. And got married. Jack has told me all along about all of her modeling success and all about her husband Lewis.

"As you both know, Jack Stampley was the sole owner of Stampley's Nursery here in town. He has left very specific instructions as to what he wants done with the ownership of the nursery now that he is no longer with us." Roger says as he looks between me and Leah. "He wants the ownership of Stampley's to be divided up between the two of you. Leah, you will have 51% and Austin you will have 49%. Jack wanted to make sure that you two know how important it is to maintain the integrity and manage the business as he would have. Austin, he believes leaving you ownership of the business will ensure that you will help to teach Leah the ins and outs of how it has been ran for decades. Leah, you have been given majority ownership because you are a Stampley.

He wants you to work very closely with Austin and keep the business thriving for decades to come."

"Why do I have to share ownership with someone I have never met?" Leah asks letting on the frustration in her voice. "How would he know what my grandfather has been doing?"

"I have worked for your grandfather for over fifteen years part time between helping at my parent's ranch. I know exactly what goes on. And furthermore, you haven't just met me. You met me every time you came to spend the summers here. I take it you don't remember." I spit out with too much anger. "I shouldn't expect a big city diva like you to remember us here in 'hickville'. Isn't that what you called it?"

She looks at me as her face turns pink and you can see the look in her eyes as she starts to remember. She looks away and says to Roger, "Are you sure about this? This is really what my grandfather wanted?"

"Since you weren't even at the funeral, what are you doing here now? He was your grandfather and you couldn't even bother to come back until you could find out what money he left you?" I say with my eyes shooting daggers at her.

"Leah was oversees doing a modeling shoot when Jack passed away. Her father was unable to get word to her quick enough for her to make it back. She just flew back yesterday. She came when I called her, just like you Austin." Roger says calmly. He thought telling me that would change my mind about her? Fat chance.

"I loved my grandfather and I loved spending time with him. I was very saddened to hear of his passing. I rushed here as soon as I could! How dare you pass judgment on me you dumb cowboy. You don't even know me." She says quickly. "Mr. Yasser, I will be at my grandfather's house if you need anything further from me."

"I will stop by the nursery tomorrow afternoon and go over the final details. You will be there correct? Both of you?" Roger asks.

"I will be there, yes, but him I couldn't tell you!" Leah says and stomps off.

"I will be there also." I say letting out the breath I wasn't aware I was holding. "So God help me I will be there. Thank you Roger." I walk outside the office towards my pickup and see Miss Priss stomping towards her sports car. That fits.

As I drive back to the 6AB Ranch of my parents, I can't help but go back over every summer I spent with Leah. She was still the stuck up little city girl that was way more high maintenance than any man wanted to deal with. Much more than I want to deal with. Ever. But seems I am stuck with her. Just my luck.

As I walk inside my Grandparents' house I begin to remember things that I had forgotten through the years. Like how I used to sit on the front porch swing where he and I would talk until the sun went down. Or we would work in the flower beds that he kept up long after grandma died. She died when I was ten but when she was alive she would bake cookies and make fresh squeezed lemonade. I started coming to stay the summers with them in Colvin when I was five years old. I stopped when I was 16 and got my first modeling gig at Saks in New York. Until his recent retirement, Dad was a prominent defense attorney in Manhattan so I was around all the great modeling agencies and close by for any auditions. Mom died when I was in middle school from breast cancer. Dad is Grandpa Stampley's only child but never liked living here in Oklahoma. He says he was made for New York and its activity. I was raised there and that's where I met my husband Lewis.

Lewis was a pitcher for the New York Yankees. I met him when my father was retained by another Yankees player to get him out of a DUI. I dropped by Dad's office one day before lunch and ran into Lewis in the elevator. Sparks flew right away and our romance was a whirlwind filled with photographers always snapping pictures of us together. I got used to having my face plastered all over the magazines and newspapers once I was offered a big modeling spot for Chanel not long after. I toured all over the world doing shoots and promotional pieces for them. I wasn't really gone overseas but the shape I was in wasn't good for me to be around so only Dad and I knew why I wasn't able to make the funeral. I knew that showing up in a wheelchair all beaten and depressed would only cause a spectacle and the media would dig into the story. That was the last thing I needed. I am mostly healed now on the outside and no one will ever know how broken I am on the inside.

I still won't talk about what happened that night. Especially not about the baby. It was a little girl. Her name would have been Shannon Elaine. Elaine after my mother. I was so happy and excited to be a mother. I would sit in her room for hours just dreaming of the day I would bring her home.

Until that one terrible day. I haven't been able to go back in that house. Especially not her room. Lewis sold the house and I couldn't be more relieved to have it gone.

I decided it was time to move on with my life but wasn't sure what I was going to do. With all of the settlement money I don't have to worry about finances, I just didn't know what I wanted to do or where I wanted to go. That was until I got a call from Roger Yasser. I packed a bag and flew to Tulsa, then rented a car and drove to Colvin this morning.

I guess Grandpa knew I needed something and that something sounds like it's a nursery and a cocky cowboy. A HOT cocky cowboy. I never would have imagined the lanky awkward boy I met at Stampley's would grow up to be so tall and handsome. I yearned to touch his arm or chest just to feel how strong he was. He is definitely one man I should stay away from. All men are bad and I need to remember that. I do not need a repeat of Lewis. All men will bend you to their will and not care how you feel or what you want. I will do as I want and not care what others think. This is my new start and I will carry on the nursery just as Grandpa wants.

But first I have to deal with him. What do I do with him? What was grandpa thinking?

\*\*\*\*\*\*\*\*\*\*\*\*\*\*\*\*\*\*

"Hey Aiden, its Austin. Got a minute?" I ask on the phone. "I need some advice. Can I swing by?"

Aiden just married his best friend from childhood, Karlie Doone about a year ago and they're expecting their first baby in a few months. I can't wait to be an uncle. I have an older brother, Aaron, younger brother, Aiden, and younger sister, Audrey. We are a big family that owns the 6AB Ranch here in Colvin.

"Sure thing man. Karlie just left for town. Come on by. I'll be in the barn." Aiden says quickly. "You're always welcome here."

I hop in my pickup and head to the AK Ranch which is Aiden's. As I do, I start to wonder what I should be doing with my life. I have always helped Mom and Dad with the 6AB and Stampley's but had always hoped to buy the nursery from Jack. Never did I dream he would give part of it to me and the other part to Leah. Leah, the big city, high fashion diva.... Good grief.

"Hey man, is she ready to have that baby today?" I ask Aiden when I find him in the horse's stall. The mare is obviously ready to pop.

"I'm thinking so." Aiden says distractedly. "What's on your mind Austin?"

"Well, I was called by Roger Yasser into his office today and he told me that Jack Stampley left me 49% ownership of the nursery." I say proudly.

"Wow. That's awesome. I know you have always wanted to own that place. When we were playing with horses and cows, you always played in the dirt with the weeds!" Aiden says teasing. "Question is who does the other 51% belong to?"

I say blowing out a breath, "His granddaughter Leah Frankle from New York."

"The granddaughter that used to come spends summers here? The one you used to have a secret crush on?" Aiden says smiling and teasing. "What's the problem here? Is she ugly now or what??"

"Very funny Aiden. She is hotter than I could have ever imagined her becoming but she is still that high society, fashion diva, high maintenance, city girl she was before if not worse!" I say disgusted.

"If you remember, that's how Karlie was when she first came back here. Just because they are that way up front, doesn't mean they are that way inside. Have you really talked to her or just the ten minutes in Yasser's office?"

"Aiden, first impressions are everything. My first impression is a lasting one believe me. She was sitting there all prim and proper with those dumb red bottom high heels on and a tight blue dress. She looked perfect. How is someone like that going to be able to keep a nursery running when you have to get your hands in the dirt?" I ask starting to show my stress level.

"Brother, you need to spend some time with her before you make any long term decisions. What exactly did you want advice on?" Aiden asks with concern in his eyes. He might be my younger brother, but he is definitely the one I go to for advice about life.

"I want to know how I go about getting her to sell me her 51% of Stampley's. I want to be the only one running it not sharing it with some diva that will want to shut it down a week after she starts because she broke a fingernail!" I am beginning to get really mad and notice that I am pacing back and forth.

"Dude, you need to take one thing at a time. You need to go talk to her. Give her a chance. She may have her own ideas and maybe not even want the nursery. Don't strong arm her into anything out of haste. You will get nothing but resistance. Remember, one step at a time." Aiden says as he slaps me on the back. "Now I have to go check on Giggles again. Yes, Giggles. That's what Karlie named the baby."

I guess the only thing to do is wait and see how it goes tomorrow. Maybe Miss Big City will have seen the light and ran back to the bright lights with her tail between those toned sexy legs. I could only hope.

"Today is the day my life starts over. Today is the day my life starts over." I repeat to myself as I open up the main gate to Stampley's Nursery. After not sleeping much last night in my old room, I am a bit on the cranky side this morning. Not just a bit, a lot.

I am thankful I have several hours alone to putter around before that pain in the butt cowboy shows up this afternoon. I am not looking forward to him blowing in here and telling me how it's going to go. I am the majority owner, not him. He better get used to that. If I only knew something about running a nursery or even plants themselves. I can't keep a cactus alive, let alone thousands of plants and flowers I have never heard of.

"You can do this. Grandpa had faith in you." I say standing in the doorway staring at the rows upon rows of plants. "He had to know what he was doing leaving me in charge."

"You sound as skeptical as I feel." I hear a low masculine voice behind me and jump sideways. "Sorry, didn't mean to scare you."

"I was just coming in here to get a feel for the place. Alone." I say annoyed by his presence. "You aren't supposed to be here until this afternoon."

"I always come in this time of day to make sure the sprinkler system is working and do anything that needs done. I have been keeping the doors open on this place since your grandfather got sick. I didn't think he would want it shut down for any reason." He says grumpily.

"Well, thank you for that but I am the majority owner now and your presence isn't needed any longer. You might as well let me buy out your 49% and you can go on about your merry cowboy way." I say with all the authority I could muster. This cowboy standing this close to me glaring only makes my blood run a little warmer than I would prefer.

"I will do no such thing, Princess. I was actually going to suggest that you let me buy out your ownership so that you can go back to your high profile lifestyle as a Yankee pitcher's wife and back to your throne in New York." He says really starting to make me mad.

"How dare you think I don't want anything to do with my family's nursery! My Grandpa left it to me along with the house so I am staying. You are the one who needs to go back to his cow patty, sweaty, and dusty existence and leave me and my nursery alone!" I am really upset now and might have been screaming.

"You are stuck with me, Princess. I have no intention of letting you run this place into the ground!" he says and stomps off. "I will be in the north greenhouse if you find yourself in need of any sweat and dusty assistance. Oh, and don't break a nail. There is only one salon here in town and I don't know if they do nails. Your crown will get wet too if you stay in here too long." he says with a mischievous smile as he shuts the door.

I spin around to ponder his aggressive words and begin to wonder what he meant by get wet. Just as I begin to take steps toward the middle of the plant rows, I feel drops on my arm. Then as if it's raining. I look up just in time to get completely soaked by the sprinklers above. Great. That is what he meant. The jerk! I run to my car knowing I have to get dry clothes from the house. I'm sure I look like a drowned rat. Thanks to Austin!

## 7

"I'm glad to find you both here. I take it things are running smoothly?" Roger asks as he enters the nursery office with Austin behind him with a smirk that says it all.

"Things are fine. I am trying to figure out the details of the business so I can start right away." Leah says with a look of hatred in her eyes as she looks my way.

"Ok well I need to have both of you sign these papers to finalize the ownership transfer. There is also one stipulation that I need to tell you about that I forgot to explain the other day." Roger says as he looks between Leah and I. "Jack has put in a clause that states that you two have to work side by side in this business for at least six months and if either of you fails to do that their ownership automatically goes to the other party. So, if you were to leave to go back to New York Leah, Austin would get your 51% and if you decide to leave Austin, Leah would get your 49%."

"So, for six months neither of us has a choice but to deal with each other. And after those six months it's a binding contract?" I question. "What if we want to buy the other out?"

"That is not possible until after the six month period." Roger says flatly.

"Great. But I do get the house right? Regardless of my ownership status in the nursery?" Leah asks.

"Yes, you get the house along with all the possessions regardless of the nursery. Is this going to be a problem between you two?" Roger asks while searching our faces. "You do understand how important it is that you two get along?"

We both nod in agreement and sign the documents sending Roger on his merry way. This is going to be the longest six months of my life.

"Well, I guess we had better get down to business." I say to Leah trying to clear the air from the sprinkler mishap earlier. Even though I knew it was time for them, I should have told her to leave. It was still funny though seeing her running out of here soaked to the core and speeding away in her little convertible. Score one for Austin.

\*\*\*\*\*\*\*\*\*\*\*\*\*\*\*\*\*\*\*

We worked in the office for several hours going over day to day operations of the nursery. Good thing I'm a quick learner. There is a lot I need to know, more than I ever dreamed possible. Sitting in this little office with my chair next to Austin's is driving me insane. I hate these feelings he's stirring up inside me every time he brushes up against my arm or leg. My skin sizzles everywhere he has touched me and I don't like it.

"Okay, enough for today. I can't see straight after looking at this computer screen all day. I'm going home but will be back tomorrow." I say standing up too quickly knocking my chair backwards. "Ooops. Will you be here tomorrow too?"

"Yes I am here for the long haul. You heard Roger, we don't have a choice princess." he says with a smirk. He is enjoying making me uncomfortable. "See you tomorrow."

I grab my purse and head to the car. My rented BMW convertible. I love this car. I just might have to go buy one like it. Wonder if there's a BMW dealership in town? I drop the top and pull away. Away from the world's most annoying cowboy.

I can see Austin in my rear view mirror standing in the door way with his arms across his chest and feet apart. Damn he is HOT! This is going to be the longest six months of my life. After living with Lewis and the media, that is saying a lot!

## 8

I decide on my way home that I am in no mood to be alone so I stop off at a baked goods store to get some muffins. The store looks so elegant, but country. It's so cute inside that I just can't help but feel at home. Ella Mae's Goodies it says on the window. That is definitely a country name. While looking at the yummy things to choose from I can hear a couple of women in the back talking about baby stuff. I look at the girl and she is definitely sporting that pregnancy glow and baby bump. I can't help but feel a sting of jealousy and pain as I see it. I should have a daughter here with me today. Should, but I don't.

I turn back to the goodies and start to fill a bag with some muffins and turnovers. Turnovers are my favorite just like Grandma used to make for me. I walk to the counter and see a young woman that looks so familiar but I can't quite place her.

As I look at her she turns her attention to me and squeals with delight, "Leah Frankle????? Is that really you??" As she rushes towards me with arms open I realize who she is.

"Karlie Doone? What are you doing here?" I say with excitement and clasp my arms around her too best I can with her pregnant belly. "I haven't seen you in a year or so!"

"I live here and this is my Mom's store. I came when dad had his first stroke. Then after we lost him I just decided to stay. Aiden and I got married and we're awaiting this little guy or gal's arrival. What are you doing here in Colvin? You're a long way from home."

"My grandpa passed away and gave me part ownership of the nursery." I say with pride.

"You are the co-owner of Stampley's? Why didn't I ever put those two names together?? Oh my goodness!! How long are you staying? We have got to get together!" She says ecstatic.

"I've decided to move here. I'm going to live in Grandpa's house on Whitten Lane. You should come by. Or you could always come to the nursery." I say happily until I realize that Austin would be there. "But the other owner will probably be there too and he is a pain in the butt."

I look at Karlie and she is smiling so big and laughing. "You must mean Austin."

"Yes, I should have known you would know who he is in this small town." I say dumbly.

"I do know him yes; he is Aiden's older brother. My brother-in-law." She says with a big smile waiting on me to understand.

"Oh my goodness, I'm sorry to insult your husband's family, it's just that he and I do not get along. We are stuck with each other and neither of us likes it." I say with distaste.

"Oh I understand. Blake men are very stubborn when they think they are right and you are wrong. I have dealt with them my whole life. Aiden and I grew up best friends but after I left here for LA we lost touch. Until I came back to help Mom. And the rest is history." She says as she puts her hands on her belly.

"I am very happy for you. Are you still taking pictures like before?" I ask. "You were always my favorite photographer."

"Not like before, I just take family pictures and play around when I have time. Aiden and I live on the AK Ranch so there is a lot there to take pictures of." She says proudly. I can really see how happy and in love she is. I get a pang of jealousy again and swallow hard trying to bury it.

"Well, why don't you come out to the ranch this evening for dinner? I would love to show you around and have you meet Aiden." She asks.

"I would love to. I didn't feel like going home to that big empty house of grandpa's yet anyway. I am so glad I ran into a familiar face." I say as I pay her mother for the goodies and head to my car. "I will follow you out there!" Maybe life won't be so bad if I have at least one friendly face around.

*******************

"Austin, why don't you come have dinner with us tonight. Karlie has a friend from LA coming tonight too." Aiden says over the phone. "Might get your mind off the nursery and your girlfriend"

"She is far from my girlfriend. I can't stand her and the same goes for her. I'll come but only because Karlie is making spaghetti and meatballs!" I say knowing this isn't a good idea. They are matchmaking and that never works out for anyone.

I shower and shave for dinner but my mind keeps wandering back to sitting next to Leah and accidentally touching her skin. Being that close to her set afire something inside me that I had been missing. I can't think about her like that though. She is a devil woman. Prissy, stuck up and hates cowboys.

After driving to the AK, I walk into the kitchen where Aiden and Karlie are and find them locked in a heated kiss. "Excuse me but get a room other than the kitchen while guests are here." I say loudly meaning to startle them.

"Oh, sorry didn't hear you come in brother." Aiden says quickly. "We will be in the barn baby. Be back in a few after we check on Giggles."

"I still can't believe you let her name it Giggles." I say shaking my head. "She has you so whooped."

"Hey, you just wait until you fall in love and see how easy it is to be whooped brother!" Aiden says punching me lightly in the arm.

"Gag me. So, tell me who this friend is of Karlie's." I say hoping to change the subject.

"She is someone she knew in the photography world. I didn't ask the specifics. Don't worry it's not a date. Karlie ran into her in Ella Mae's today and invited her out so they could catch up." Aiden says trying to sound like he didn't have matchmaking in mind. But I know better.

"Mom said to tell you she's going to come by Stampley's soon to place that large order for the new flower beds she had Dad do by the cabin." Aiden says looking at the horse in the stall. "I think she wants to meet the girl that is causing you to lose your cool so quickly."

"Oh great, her matchmaking and yours, should be so NOT fun."

We walk back into the kitchen not aware that the other dinner guest had arrived. As we round the corner we see Karlie animatedly telling the new guest a story and then I heard her laugh. That's the moment it clicked and I knew that red hair and that tight butt. Those gorgeously hot legs and feet belonged to the one woman I didn't want to see tonight. And did not want to be stuck having a cozy family meal in my brother's dining room. I have to be near her at the nursery but this space was off limits.

"Oh hey guys, I want you to meet Leah. Well, Austin you already know her but Aiden you don't. She is Jack Stampley's granddaughter." Karlie says towards him with a smirk on her face. Yep, a set up.

"Well, you're the woman that has my big brother all in a tizzy. Nice to put a face to the situation." Aiden says with a grin.

"Thank you but your brother and I don't get along so I will be on my way back to town. Thank you for inviting me Karlie, maybe another time." She says. "When he isn't here preferably."

And with that she walked out. I'm not sure how I'm supposed to feel about that but judging from the looks on my brother and sister-in-laws faces they are expecting me to go after her and beg her to stay. Awww damn it!

I run and catch her just as she's backing away from the house. Stepping in front of her car the headlights flash on me and she slams on the brakes. "Do you have a death wish or what? You do know that if you die I get 100% control of the nursery right?"

"I'm sorry for being so rude in the house. I promise to be nice if you'll just come back inside. Aiden and Karlie really want you to stay. And I'll never hear the end of it if you don't." I say choking on the words. "And so do I." That didn't taste any better.

She looks at me quizzically. She must be wondering if I am serious. I walk up to her door and reach in to put the car in park. I pull the keys out of the ignition and walk back to the house. All the while I hear her yelling and cussing at me from the driveway. A little smile crosses my lips.

## 9

How could he do this to me? He said he would be nice but then he stole my keys. What a child! Stomping back towards the house I can see Karlie and Aiden watching from the front window. I smile and step inside trying to calm myself. This is going to be a long night. That jerk.

"Leah was one of my first models when I was interning for Gerry." Karlie says halfway through dinner to break up the silence, "Then once I got KAB going I met her again on a shoot in Paris. She was always one of my favorites to work with. We always got together whenever we were in the same city. Now I am so very happy that she will be living here in Colvin and Gerry won't believe it either!"

"You were my favorite too Karlie. I would always ask who the photographer was first before taking a gig. Once I signed on with Chanel though they usually didn't like me asking. They thought it was something I didn't need to know but Gerry would always try to get you for me." I say before reaching for a roll.

As I do, Austin reaches in too and our hands touch making sparks fly like fireworks and I jerk my hand back in shock. That has never happened when I've touched anyone else, especially not Lewis. I look at Austin and he seems to be pondering the same thing.

"How long after you started modeling did you get married?" Asks Aiden. "Are you still married?" I have a feeling that is a loaded question and I shoot a glance to Austin to find him glaring at his brother.

"I met Lewis at my father's law firm. Dad was working with a friend of Lewis'. We got married three years after I started modeling." I say and clear my throat not wanting to talk about him. "No, I am not still married."

"I'm sorry that was kinda personal." Karlie says hitting Aiden and shooting him with a dirty look. "How are things going at the nursery?"

Austin and I both look at each other and let out matching sighs. That was all that was needed to get the point across that neither of us was happy with the nursery situation or wanted to talk about it.

\*\*\*\*\*\*\*\*\*\*\*\*\*\*\*\*\*\*

"Thank you for inviting me tonight. It was great to meet your husband and see you again." I hear Leah say to Karlie as they hug good-bye and Karlie tells her, "Don't be a stranger!"

I roll my eyes and shake my head. Great she is going to be a permanent pain in my butt even outside the nursery.

"Are you waiting for a goodnight kiss?" Aiden asks from the kitchen doorway where he stands with arms crossed and an evil smirk on his face. Of course he would find all of this comical.

"Very funny. You know we don't get along. No more matchmaking, got it?" I spit out and shoot daggers with the look I give him and walk out the door to the barn.

\*\*\*\*\*\*\*\*\*\*\*\*\*\*\*\*\*\*

"I can't believe Karlie set that whole dinner up with Austin and me! She knows we don't get along!" Hmph! I am so upset I don't realize I've been pressing a little too hard on the gas pedal. And I am not sure where I am.

Karlie's directions were easy to follow getting out there in the daylight but now in the dark not so easy. Great, I think I'm lost. Completely lost in the dark country side of a strange town, wonderful.

I slow my car at the next dirt road but don't recognize it. She told me to turn on II and JJ and this one is Q. Wow I really am lost! Where the heck do I go now? I guess if I turn around and go back down the way I came maybe I'll find the right road. I don't want to call Karlie and tell her I'm lost. Word will get back to Austin and I won't live this down for a long time. He already thinks I am too big city for Colvin.

I've driven another ten minutes and still nothing familiar. Great. I pull my car over at the next spot I can find, put it in park and take a deep breath.

"Don't freak out Leah, don't freak out." Another deep breath and reach for my phone.

No service. Imagine that! This night could not get any worse!

I unbuckle my seat belt and roll the driver's window down. Fresh air might do my frazzled nerves some good. Breathing in and out I begin to relax after a few minutes. I can hear coyotes howling in the darkness and makes the hair stand up on the back of my neck. I quickly roll up the window and turn on the radio. Surely someone will come along sooner rather than later that will stop and help me. Someone without a record or a need to hack me into a million pieces. What did I have to go there for? This is Colvin not New York!

# 10

After helping Aiden with the new horses he got, I head towards town. I have work to do at the nursery but I can't help but let my mind wander to the other guest that was invited by Karlie tonight. She and Aiden's matchmaking needs to stop. Leah doesn't like me anymore than I like her.

"Hey Austin ,can you swing by the far west pasture over by Grand's place to make sure no more cows have gotten out? Jan Grand just called saying she thinks some were out but she might be seeing some coyotes. Thanks man, appreciate it."

I hang up the phone and head west where I will soon lose service and not see a house for miles. This is where we get the name "the boonies".

Driving along and listening to George Strait on the radio, I soon come upon a set of brake lights alongside the road about a mile ahead. Who in the world would be this far out?

As I get closer I realize it's a small convertible BMW. And I know this car. And the driver. Leah. What is this big city girl doing out here in the dark in the middle of nowhere?

I pull my pickup alongside the road behind her and turn off the engine and unbuckle slowly unsure of how the next few minutes are going to play out.

\*\*\*\*\*\*\*\*\*\*\*\*\*\*\*\*\*\*\*\*

I watch the rear view mirror as headlights are starting to come towards me. A mixture of happy and fear swarm through me as I see them get bigger and bigger. Please be someone nice and willing to give me directions out of this jam I've gotten myself into. The butterflies and dread start to grow stronger the closer the lights get. I reach over and hit the lock button even though I know it's already locked.

They are pulling over. Good, they can send me on my way back to town. I hope they're nice and not killers.

The door's opening and I see it's a man getting out. No one is with him. My heartbeat is racing, I am so scared. I lean my head back and take a deep breath as the man comes closer and closer to my driver's door. His headlights just went out and I can't really see him anymore with all this darkness. I have a key chain with a flashlight that I can use to shine in his face to get a look at him before I roll the window down.

As I lean down to get the flashlight off the key ring, I hear a knock at my window. Luckily, I feel the flashlight with my right hand. I click it on as I lift it to shine into this strange man's face.

Only to find out that I recognize him. Of course it's the last man I would ever want to come to my rescue! Austin! Ugh! I'm never going to hear the end of this! I am tempted to just ignore him. But I want to go home so I roll the window down and look everywhere but at him.

"Leah, what are you doing out here alone this late?"

'I just pulled over to make a call."

"There's no call service in this area."

"No kidding."

"Why are you even out this far west? The AK is about 10 miles the other way."

"What are you doing out here then?"

"Aiden asked me to check on a herd of cows over here a little farther up the road. I only stopped because I thought you needed help."

"Well, I don't thanks." I shouldn't have said that. I need directions but he won't let me ever live this down if I ask for help. But no one else will probably come along until morning. Ugh!

"Ok, sorry. Drive safe, I have cows to check on." And he walks back to his pickup and drives away.

What did I send him away for? He might have been my only hope of getting back to town. Ugh!

\*\*\*\*\*\*\*\*\*\*\*\*\*\*\*\*\*\*\*

What is her issue? I was only trying to help. Shoot me for being nice. I can't win with her no matter what I do.

Driving away I watch her car get smaller and smaller in the rear view. She hasn't started it yet. Why? What is that crazy girl up to now? Surely she will be gone when I come back.

Fifteen minutes or so later, after checking on the herd, I start my pickup and head back the way I came. Back by where Leah was stopped earlier.

Eventually I start to see my lights hitting a car along the road. What is she still doing there? The closer I get the clearer I can see that she is standing outside of it alongside the road, so I pull off into the ditch. I put the pickup in park and see her start across the road towards me so I roll my window down unsure of what's going on. Is she going to scream at me for being civil again?

*******************

Walking across this road to where Austin is parked is like the worst walk of shame I could imagine. I was so snotty to him earlier and told him I didn't need help. I was such a jerk and I'm surprised he stopped now. Not sure that I would have if the roles were reversed.

"Ok, I lied. I don't know where I am and need directions back to town." That was rough to spit out. He is smiling that cocky smile that drives me insane too!

"Why didn't you just say so the first time I stopped?"

"I don't know. Embarrassed I guess. Will you help me or not?"

"Just follow me. I'm headed back to the nursery anyways."

"What are you going there so late for?"

"Just wanted to work on a few things while we weren't open."

"And when I wasn't there."

"Yes maybe that too. Just follow me to town then you can turn off at main and I'll continue to the nursery."

"Thanks. I really do appreciate it. And I'm sorry about before!"

I turn to walk back to my car feeling very ashamed of what a nit whit I am. Not paying attention on the roads out here in the dark and then being a jerk to the one person who stopped to check on me. But it just had to be Austin! Ugh!

******************

Watching Leah walk back to her car makes me smile. I just heard that girl apologize and admit she was wrong all within a few minute's time. That had to have be tough on her little 5'7" ego.

I put my pickup in gear and start towards town continually looking in the rear view mirror like a child waiting on Santa.

After driving for almost twenty minutes, we hit the edge of town and find ourselves nearing her turn off. I see her car signal left but then turn it off as she passes on by the turn and continues behind me all the way to the nursery.

I park and get out but stop short of her driver's door as she steps out.

"You missed your turn back there."

"I know, but I didn't feel like going home. I thought maybe I would come get work done too or just hang out here that is if you don't mind my being here."

"Nope. You're good. You're half owner too. Can't keep you out." Smiling a genuine smile I surprise myself when I realize that I really am glad she's here. I didn't want to be alone either.

"I'll just be in the office if you need me."

"Ok. I'll be in the potting sheds out back. Those new bags of fertilizer came in and I need to get them separated into each shed. "

I walk away leaving her standing there with an unsure look on her face. She looked as if she might want to say something else but didn't.

*******************

I can't help but wonder why I continued on to the nursery instead of going home. I don't have any work that is so pressing that needs done tonight. Come to think of it, why is Austin here tonight? The fertilizer can be done anytime. Maybe he didn't want to go home alone either.

After looking at these papers at least fifty times I realize that I am not getting anything done and can't quit wondering what Austin is doing out there. I can't do this. No man's worth this.

Finally, I stand up and grab my things. I lock the front door and head to my car. Enough is enough. I can find better things to do at home than sit around wondering what that dumb cowboy is doing.

\*\*\*\*\*\*\*\*\*\*\*\*\*\*\*\*\*\*

After finishing up my tasks I came to do, I walk up front in hopes that Leah is still in the office. We might have finally made it over that awkward and unfriendly hump where we could be friends.

But, as I near the office, I see the lights are all out and her car is gone. She left without even a word. Ok, maybe I was wrong.

## 11

After dinner at Karlie's last night it hits me that I might have a distorted view of cowboys, probably from watching too many movies. I expected her and Aiden's house to be a shack all dusty and old. Was I ever wrong about that. The house was large and modern. It was all pristine and the grounds were as if they were in the Upper East Side. I still can't believe the kitchen in that house. It was as big as my first apartment in New York.

Pulling up to the nursery I see that Austin has beaten me here today. He looks up from the tailgate he was sitting plants onto only to frown at me. I see last night didn't help his feelings about me. Why should I care how he feels about me? I have rubbed elbows with New York's richest and I may actually be one of them but he doesn't know the first thing about me or New York.

I get out of my car and head for the office. He looks at me and asks, "Not even going to say hello Princess?"

"Nope. With the look I got from you when I pulled up, I got the message." I say and stick my nose in the air and walk off. Maybe that wasn't the way to react since he already thinks I'm stuck up.

"Good morning business partner." I yell as I slip inside the door and shut it. Making sure I get the last word in.

*******************

Dragging the watering hose from aisle to aisle in the nursery, I hear the door chime letting me know a customer has arrived. I drop the nozzle and walk towards the front while wiping my hands on my jeans.

"Hi there. Can I help you find something?"

"I'm looking for my little flower."

"Um, which flower would that be? I'm sure I can help you find it."

"My daughter. Leah. I'm Mike Stampley. And you must be Austin. I have heard so much about you for so many years. Thank you for all you have done and continue to do for Stampley's. Especially Dad's last few years.

"Oh sir, I'm sorry I didn't recognize you. And it was definitely my pleasure; I have such a passion for the nursery."

"You were a child the last time I was here. Don't worry about it."

"Leah is in the back potting shed working with the Gerber Daisies I believe. You can go right through that door there and go left when you reach the end of that hallway. The last shed door should be open and you will find her."

"Oh thanks Austin. We need to have dinner while I'm here. I'd like to talk to you a little more about Dad and the nursery. Nice to see you again."

"Thank you sir, you too."

Leah's Dad walks away and I wonder what exactly he is doing here after all these years. He hasn't come around at all since I was a teenager running up and down these aisles. He must be here to check on Leah. Nice guy, I know where he got it; he reminds me a lot of Jack.

## 12

Gerber Daisies were my Mother's favorite flowers when she was alive. Every time I see one I think of her. Even as she was so sick in the end, Dad would bring them to her and she would just smile the biggest smile. I didn't realize how much I had missed seeing them until I got the order in yesterday. I insisted to Austin that I be the one to work with them. Grandpa always kept the little pink roses for me that I liked as a child and then these for my Mom. It is so nice to see that he still has them even after all these years even though we hadn't been around.

I should have come around a little more often. I know that now. I only wish I would've realized that before he passed away. I don't really remember why I didn't, just that this small town wasn't somewhere I wanted to visit on my time off from school after I got busy with high school, sports, boys and then modeling. Dad hasn't come back here either, I'm sure I'm not the only one feeling guilty.

"How's my little flower?" I hear from behind me and instantly draw a huge grin because there is only one man in the world that calls me that.

"Hi Dad! What are you doing here? What a surprise! I didn't know you were coming." I rush over to him and give him a hug. It feels so good to have his strong arms scooping me up like he has since I was a child.

"That handsome young man up front told me you were back here. He told me you're playing with Mama's favorite flowers."

"You must be talking about Austin."

"Yes dear, Austin." I don't like that smile on his face, almost ornery.

"I was just reminiscing about Mama before you came in. I was remembering how you used to bring her these in the end and how sweet she would smile. It always brightened her day to see her favorite flowers from her favorite man."

"It's been awhile since I've seen ones this pretty. She would have loved them. Bringing her flowers was the only thing I could do to make her feel better. Even if it were only for a few moments."

"Yes, I told Austin I would deal with these because I hadn't thought about them in years and I wanted to change that. For Mama."

"I saw that Grandpa has the little pink roses you used to love too. And the young man you used to fancy."

"What are you talking about? I never liked Austin like that. He and I have never gotten along. Still don't really."

"That is what you have said but anyone around you two could tell even at a young age how much you two clicked. You know Grandpa always hoped you two would get married."

"Oh good grief Dad that is insane. Until I came back here and Austin introduced himself, I didn't even remember him. I still don't really remember him. Not like he seems to remember me and my time here. That was a long time ago and it needs to stay that way."

I put the flowers back and motion for Dad to head out the door. I shut it and he wraps his left arm around my shoulders as we walk back towards the front of the nursery. I am so happy Dad surprised me with this visit. I am afraid to ask why he is here though. He hasn't been back here in probably fifteen years except for the funeral. So why now?

"Let's go in the office and sit down. Do you want some water or something?"

"Sure. I'll meet you in there."

Walking to the back room to get Dad's water I hear Austin yell from the other end of the store room. "Your Dad find you?"

"Yep thanks." I say and grab the water bottle out of the fridge and head back to the office. I think Austin is still talking but I ignore him and keep on.

*******************

She just ignored that I was talking to her. Or maybe she didn't hear me. Either way I guess I better swing by the office and tell her again before I head home for the day. I walk towards the office and I can hear her father talking to her about growing up in the nursery.

"Excuse me a second, Leah I wanted to let you know that we will have a large delivery in the morning so I will be in early. I'm going home now though. It was so nice to see you again Mr. Stampley. Have a good night."

"You too Austin, please call me Mike. Why don't you have dinner with Leah and me tonight? I would love to hear some of the stories about this place and my Dad. You wouldn't mind would you Leah?"

"Um, no I guess not. Unless you have something else to do Austin." She looks almost pained with that answer.

"No, I don't have any plans. If you're sure it's ok Leah I'd love to join you and talk about Jack and Stampley's."

"It's settled then. We can go to Sally's if it's still open. Is it?"

"Yep it is. Austin, we'll be there about six o'clock."

"Ok, see you two then. Thanks for the invite. Bye."

Dinner with Leah and her dad. What was I thinking? She and I don't like each other. Dinner with her father is going to be worse than spending the evening at the AK with Aiden and Karlie. At least this time I know Leah won't get lost driving home. That brings a small chuckle and smile. She hasn't been quite as high and mighty since that night. Not exactly my biggest fan but not my biggest enemy either. Maybe tonight could help that. I wouldn't mind getting to know her better, would make working with her a lot easier.

\*\*\*\*\*\*\*\*\*\*\*\*\*\*\*\*\*\*\*

"Dad are you insane? Why did you just invite that man to have dinner with us?"

"I like that boy and I would really like to hear his stories. What are you so upset about?"

"I don't want to have dinner with Austin. Ever. I don't understand why tonight had to be the night you invited the enemy."

"The enemy? Why in the world do you view him like that? Your Grandpa wrote his will this way for a reason."

"To torture me I am beginning to think. Austin and I do not get along. As long as we stay far away from each other we are better off."

"Well, you can do this for your father at least can't you? I feel guilty that I haven't been here all these years. After being back I feel even worse. I missed out on a lot. Especially time with my own Dad."

"Oh whatever. But don't expect me to be happy about any of this dinner idea. I will just sit there and listen. I will not carry on a conversation with that man."

"Oh Leah, you are being dramatic. He isn't that bad. I don't see what the problem is."

"I'm done talking about this Dad. Done. Now go on to the house and get unpacked while I wrap things up here. I'll be home before dinner to shower and change. Then we will go meet your new best friend."

"I love you my beautiful flower. See you soon."

"Bye Dad. Love you too and thanks for coming to see me. Even if you are meddling." Then he walks out the door and back to his rental car. I don't know what he was thinking asking Austin to meet us for dinner. Why would anyone want to have dinner with Austin? Not I. Maybe I can fake a headache and get out of it. Let them have their boy time. Dad will never let that happen.

"I have to go Aiden, I can't help tonight. I'm meeting Mike and Leah at Sally's for dinner. Yes, Leah's Dad is in town. I think he just got here today. No, she wasn't happy about the invitation. Of course I'm going. He wants to talk about Jack and the nursery. I happen to love to talk most about those two things. I know, tell Karlie I'll be nice. She needs to tell her friend that. She's the one that isn't nice. You know me, I am always nice. Ha ha not funny. My life hasn't been scandalous like yours little brother. Ha! Back at ya. Ok, well I'll talk to you in the morning. No, don't call me later and tell her no I won't call after dinner. If she's so curious she can call Leah. Ok, gotta shower. Bye."

I hang up my cell phone and shake my head knowing Aiden and Karlie are getting way too much enjoyment out of this Leah situation. I don't see what it is they think is going to happen here. We don't like each other. I am only going to dinner to talk to her dad. That's it.

As I walk into Sally's, Mike smiles but Leah frowns when they see that I did come. She looks really upset. Maybe I shouldn't be here.

"Austin, so glad you could make it. I'm really looking forward to this dinner."

"Same here Mike. Leah, how are you?"

"I'm fine thanks. Where do you want to sit? Karlie tells me this is the best spot."

"That works."

"Austin, tell me what you like best on this menu. It's been ages since I have had any of Sally's good cooking."

"I like her mushroom and Swiss burger the best. My brothers and sister used to come in here every day after school and Sally would know before we got seated what we wanted. Still does actually because she just winked at me." I smile knowing she is probably already making the burger.

"That's Leah's favorite burger too. Have you eaten one here Flower?"

"Yes, that's what I was going to order. I love them too. I agree they are the best thing on the menu." She says that without making eye contact with me or her Dad.

"Interesting that we like the same burger. I might have to bring you lunch someday now that I know what you like."

"That's not necessary. I can come get my own burger."

"Ok ok, change of subject. How long have you been working at Stampley's Austin?"

"Since I was a teenager. Probably twenty five years. Wow. Am I really old enough to say that?"

"Time flies. Are you married Austin? Kids?"

"No sir. Haven't found the right girl yet. Not many to choose from here in Colvin."

"I hear ya there. I found Leah's mom when I started college at Harvard. She was a cheerleader at NYU. She was so beautiful but she hated me from the start. It took me probably a year to wear her down and get her to go out with me."

"Sounds familiar. Your daughter hates me."

"I don't hate you. And we aren't dating you moron."

"I didn't mean it like that Leah. Geez."

"Ok ok, another change of subject. Your family still owns the big ranch north of town right?"

"Yes, the 6AB. My younger brother bought a hundred acres from them about seven or eight years ago. Now he and his wife live there and they do most of the 6AB Breeds horse breeding program."

"Is that where you live? Still on the 6AB?"

"No, I rent a house here in town. It's closer to the nursery and that's where I spend most of my time so it didn't seem logical to be commuting from the ranch to the nursery every day. When Jack got sicker I always felt as if I needed to be handy in case he needed me."

"I can't tell you how grateful I am that he had someone like you there for him. I have to admit that I feel so guilty because I should have been the one here. I let my own life and feelings cloud my judgment and now I have to deal with the consequences. He was very lucky to have you around."

"It was never a big deal to me. He was a very special person and the nursery is like my second home. I was actually in talks with him to one day buy the nursery from him. That's why I was so shocked about the ownership split."

"Now that you are part owner along with my daughter, do you have any plans?"

"I have a lot of ideas but Leah and I have to get to know each other and learn how to do this together before we can move forward with any changes. At least I hope she agrees with that."

"Yes, I agree with that. We can barely stand each other long enough to pass through the hallway together let alone try to work together on a project."

"And why is it that you two despise each other so much? I really can't figure this one out. Since you brought it up."

"Dad, let's not get into this right now please."

"I would rather not too if you don't mind Mike. Our food should be here soon. Why don't you tell us why you decided to come down after all these years?"

"I wanted to see Leah and I wanted to see the nursery. Like I said before I feel guilty for abandoning Dad and Stampley's. I was only here long enough for Dad's funeral and didn't see a reason to stick around very long. I guess I thought that if I came down here I could move on. I think that might actually be right."

"Whatever makes you feel better Dad. You're welcome here anytime and for as long as you want. Grandpa would be happy to know you're here."

"Flower I appreciate that but I'm not going to be here very long. I leave day after tomorrow. Have a lot to do since I'm retiring and moving to Martha's Vineyard."

"Retiring. How exciting. What is it you're retiring from?"

"Law firm. I'm an attorney."

"Oh I knew that. I think Jack told me. He was very proud of you and proud of Leah's modeling career."

"Thank you for saying that but can we please stop talking? Here's our food." Leah snaps out.

Our food did arrive and none of us said another word except about the food the rest of the night. That made the evening even more awkward. I shouldn't have come I guess. Leah was very uncomfortable and poor Mike couldn't seem to say anything to cheer her up. I will remember this the next time he invites me.

## 14

"Well that was disastrous Dad! Why did you have to invite him?"

"I'm not going there again Leah. It's over, now I would like to get some rest. I will see you in the morning. Goodnight, love you."

"I love you too Dad. Thanks for coming to see me. See you tomorrow. I will be gone early for that delivery but will see you after. Sleep well."

"Ok night."

That was a horrible dinner. Why do I let Austin make me so mad? What is it about him that just rubs me the wrong way over and over again? He is like no other man I have ever met. Nice, polite, thoughtful, and of course handsome. I am human. Of course I see that he is hot. But I am not looking for a man right now. Even if one as hot as Austin is so near ALL THE TIME.... Why did Grandpa have to shove us together like this? All the men around here are insane. Every last one of them.

"Karlie, I don't know what to do or think about your brother in law. He drives me crazy!" I say into my cell phone once I walk into my bedroom.

"I take it dinner didn't go well?"

"Karlie, it isn't funny. We fought like always and ended up not talking for most of the meal. Awkward silence. Even my Dad."

"You two like to fight that is for sure."

"I don't like fighting with him; it's what always happens when we are around each other. He makes me so mad!"

"I don't understand why you two can't get along. You are both great people. But together you are a menace."

"Why did I call you again?"

"Because you wanted to gossip about your night."

"Dad seems to think Austin and I are destined or whatever he's clearly nuts."

"Your dad's a very smart man."

"Blah blah. Anyway, how are you feeling?"

"Fat. Aiden told me tonight that my belly got twice the size overnight."

"That's not nice. Men are such pigs. Especially Blake men."

"I see how you turned that back around to Austin.  You kinda like him don't ya?"

"No.  Can't stand him.  Did you not just hear me say he is a pig?"

"Uh huh.  I don't believe you."

"Good-bye Karlie, I needed a friend, not a matchmaker."

"You know you love me Leah!"

"I wonder why sometimes."

Hanging up my cell phone I can't help but smile knowing Karlie is sitting on the couch with a pillow under her knees probably having to listen to Aiden pick at her about not sleeping.  They have the perfect relationship.  I can only hope for one like that one day.

For some reason the picture in my head shifted from Aiden and Karlie to me and- AUSTIN?  What?  That can't be.  I must be tired.  And delusional.  That is the only explanation.  I don't like him and he doesn't like me.  Ugh I think it's beyond time for bed.  Get this day over with.

## 15

The next morning at the nursery, I've been in the office for about thirty minutes when an older woman walks in through the door and asks if I am Leah. I look up at her and see the familiar eyes of the man outside. This must be his mother. Has to be.

I stand and extend my hand towards her, "Hi, I'm Leah. You must be Austin's mother. He looks a lot like you."

"Well, thank you dear I'm Amelia Blake. Austin is my middle son. And biggest pain in the rear!" she says laughing. "As I hear you have found out first hand."

"Yes ma'am I have found that out. Actually, the first day in the attorney's office. Or years ago if I think back far enough." I say smiling back remembering his disdain for me. "But I'm from New York so he doesn't scare me."

"Glad to hear it. He really isn't all that bad. He has a big heart and loves this nursery as much as he does the ranch. I was very pleased to hear that Jack had given him part ownership after all the years and hard work he has put in here." Amelia said with a slight smile.

"I am glad to hear Grandpa had good help. Now, what can I do for you Mrs. Blake?" I ask trying to get back on track.

"Please call me Amelia. Mrs. Blake is AJ's mother. I have an order of new bed plants that I came to pay for and pick up. That is what Austin is loading into his pickup. Could you tell me how much I owe you?" Amelia says kindly as she sits down in front of my desk.

I fumble through the computer program to find the order she is talking about thankful I didn't need Austin's help. "Thank you so much for your order Amelia. It's gratifying to know that Stampley's has such loyal customers even with Grandpa being gone."

"I have been coming here since I first moved to Colvin. I wouldn't go anywhere else. Thank you and go easy on Austin. He'll come around." She says and exits.

"Easy on him…. Yeah right. He hates me too." I say to myself.

"I don't hate you Leah." I startle once again by him sneaking up on me.

"Would you stop sneaking up on me? You do it on purpose. What do you want?" I ask with too much annoyance in my voice. "And don't lie about hating me, it's written all over your face."

"I'm going to the 6AB, which is my family's ranch, to deliver these plants. Wanted to know if you would like to join me. You could see how we do that side of things. We can close up for a while."

Just seeing him squirm while asking the question made me want to go even more, "Of course, that sounds like a good idea." I do need to know the delivery side, right?

*******************

The drive to the ranch was torture. I didn't know what to say to her and couldn't quit looking at her in profile. She is so gorgeous it's hard not to. I even caught her looking at me a couple times.

"It's beautiful out here Austin."

"It's been in our family for 300 years. Aiden bought his 100 acres from our parents and Aaron lives in Denver. It's just Audrey still here on the ranch with the folks." Why did I just say all that? Idiot.

"So, is your father going to stay in New York or come back here?"

"He loves the big city life too much to come back here. He said he always felt like a fish out of water here. Although after being here myself I'm not sure why he felt that way. I love it here. So beautiful and peaceful." She said surprising me that she felt that way.

"I'm shocked to hear you say that. I figured you would miss the shopping, fashion, and endless activity of the big city. How can we compete with Chanel and Louis Vuitton?"

I see her get angry and cross her arms over her chest. As she does it makes her cleavage come into full view in that silky yellow top she has on. I make myself look away before I get drawn into something that is clearly wrong.

"How dare you say something like that! You don't even know me! I am not the snobby rich girl you make me out to be Austin. Have you ever even asked me why I was here? No, so keep your opinions about me to yourself!" she says angrily and turns herself towards the door.

"I'm sorry Leah. You're right, I was wrong to judge you before really knowing you. I'll try to keep my opinions to myself and stay out of your way. We have a long six months together; we better make the best of it." I say knowing I messed up and feeling guilty. "Truce?"

"I'll think about it."

Later in the week I'm still dumbfounded that the 6AB Ranch could be so outstanding. I never thought cowboys could live like that. I guess I can't blame Austin for thinking I was a spoiled rich girl from the big city when I thought he was a cow patty throwing hick.

Knowing I was going home alone, I decided to stop off at Sally's Café and get something to go. I know I'm in way over my head with the nursery. How did grandpa think I was going to be able to run this? Oh yeah, with Austin's help, that's how. Hmph! I need Austin and that's going to kill me to have to admit.

As I walk inside I feel my phone vibrate in my pocket. I take it out and see it's a text from Karlie.

*Hey you! Wanna have a girl's night?*

A girl's night? She is pregnant how would that work?

*How does a girl's night work pregnant?*

And before I know it I see her and another blond standing on the other side of the café window holding tons of shopping bags and big smiles. They rush in as I place my order to go. Karlie adds their orders to mine and we sit at the counter on barstools awaiting the food's arrival. This is a little awkward because I haven't a clue whom this other girl is. Why would Karlie bring someone I didn't know to our girl's night?

After getting our food we head to my house. Funny how comfortable it is for me to say Grandpa's house is mine after only being in town for little over a week.

Letting the girls into the house was like I had done it forever. Like I had lived here forever and had Karlie over a million times. A lot of the furniture is old and not my style so when I took the rental car back to Tulsa I bought a new pickup. Having one will allow me to deliver plants for the nursery and I can haul new furniture that I find in town. And I won't have to do anymore ride alongs with Austin.

"Leah, this is Audrey. She is Aiden and Austin's little sister. I thought it would be good for you two to get to know each other and we can all become really good friends, you don't mind do you?"

"Of course not, it's very nice to meet you Audrey. Please come in and make yourselves comfortable. Well as comfortable as you can on this old furniture."

"This house is gorgeous Leah. Nothing like our house, this one has so much character. I can't wait to see what you do to all of it! You need to find you a husband and have a bunch of kids to fill it up!" Karlie says with so much excitement and a wink.

I, on the other hand, tense up when she says husband and kids. After what I went through with Lewis and the baby I don't think I will ever be ready for that again. She must have sensed my hesitance and said, "You do want a family don't you?"

"I have done the whole marriage thing and it wasn't all rainbows and sunshine." I say trying to pull away from the hurtful subject. "So how does this girl's night begin?"

"How about we play truth or dare?" Karlie asks looking mischievous at Audrey. This can't be good.

"Never played but I'll give it a go." I say reluctantly, "You first."

"Truth." She says quickly.

"Um let me think." I say really trying to come up with something good. "What do you really think of your brother in law Austin?"

"Oh good one missy." She says smiling and laughing, "I think he is the second biggest pain in the rear but is also a very thoughtful and loyal man. If I wasn't in love with Aiden I would want Austin! Ok your turn. Audrey you ask the question."

"I guess truth too." I say wishing I knew in advance her question.

"What do you really think of my brother Austin?" she says with a big smile getting even bigger and wiggling her eyebrows at me, "And you have to tell the truth!"

"I should have known she wouldn't keep that quiet. Um, well as you well know he is good looking but a big pain." I say quickly not looking at either woman.

"More detail than that! You aren't getting off that easy!" Karlie screams with laughter in her voice.

"Oh boy. This does not leave this house. Got it?" I ask meaning it whole heartedly. "I think he is HOT and since I first saw him have dreamed about putting my hands on that strong chest of his and what that cocky mouth of his would taste like. Ok are you happy now? If a word of this gets back to him I will kill you both, got it?"

Shocked Karlie stands up screaming, "I knew it!!! I knew it!!! I told you Audrey!! I told Aiden too that there were sparks so big it could ignite the house when you two were there for dinner."

"Well nothing will ever come from it. He hates me and thinks I am some snobby New Yorker." I say pouting.

"You act like one most of the time." Karlie says trying to smile and not upset me. "You wear your designer clothes, wear your hair and makeup perfect and drive a BMW convertible. Well, not anymore but you did."

"I don't think the way you look has anything to do with it. Austin has never really thought of anything other than the nursery. You being part owner now scares him that he will lose it all. And you are hot so it's knocking him off kilter." Audrey says standing and trying to get Karlie to sit back down.

"But I have a truck now. What am I supposed to do about my clothes? They are all I have. I have tried wearing the most sensible ones to the nursery. Am I supposed to go buy a whole new wardrobe just to make Austin happy?" I ask thinking I know where that would lead. Back to being a trophy wife again and I wasn't ok with it then and I won't be that now either. But this might not be me anymore either.

"We will take you shopping downtown. If you quit wearing all that makeup and smiled a little more you would be a whole new person." Karlie says putting her arms around me and Audrey.

"I just don't know who I am anymore. I have been lost for so long I'm not sure who it is I'm supposed to be now. Will you help me?" I ask wiping tears from my eyes.

"Of course we will honey. You are my closest friend and I am so happy to have you here. So happy to help you be happy like me." She says as she gets out the nail polish for manicures. I can't believe I just said all of that to Karlie and more importantly to Austin's sister. This can't be good.

## 17

I am always on edge around Leah trying not to feel things for her that I feel. She has been hanging around with Karlie and Audrey a lot according to Aiden. Which I should be glad because maybe she needed a friend like Aiden had said. It's natural to have concern for your business partner, right?

"Mom, how are things today at the ranch? There's a big storm coming. Any help needed out there?" I ask after she answers the phone.

"Austin you know we have it all under control here. You should be more worried about Leah and that nursery you two own. Make sure things are able to weather this major storm coming our way." Mom says before going on to tell me about the baby shopping she and Karlie did. Like I care about that stuff. "Make sure Leah is ok too with the storm. Nothing like this in New York."

"Bye mom." I hang up and shake my head. Always thinking of everyone.

I dial Karlie's number and wait for her to answer.

"Hey Karlie, its Austin. Is Leah with you?" I ask knowing it's going to cause her eyebrows to rise with me asking about her. "I need to have her meet me at the nursery. A storm's coming and we have some stuff to do beforehand."

"I'll call her and tell her for you Austin." And with that she hung up. Maybe I should just give her my number and get hers. We are partners. Even if it's just business.

I walk into the office at the nursery and scribble down my name and numbers on a sticky note. Leaving it on the desk I walk out to start the storm preparations.

Not hearing her pull up she was the one to sneak up on me today.

"Karlie says we have to get ready for a storm?" she says from behind me with a smirk knowing she startled me this time.

I turn around to see her but am blown away by the woman standing in front of me. Gone is the high fashion, snobby rich girl. In front of me is a beautiful red headed woman that looks as if she were to have been born and bred here in Oklahoma. Her hair was in a ponytail, very little makeup on and boots with her tight jeans and tee shirt.

Knowing that I must be standing with my mouth wide open, I put my hand over my mouth and shake my head. "Where did you come from and what did you do with my business partner Leah?"

"Very funny you dumb cowboy now what do we need to do?" she says quite annoyed with my reaction to her appearance change. What did she expect? She's a complete knockout!

"I can't help it if you look so different." Not able to look away I say to her and wave my hands as to show my meaning.

"Can't a girl dress down for a change without being ridiculed for it?" she snaps.

"I am far from ridiculing you Leah. You look amazing Princess." I say dumbfounded to know I just said that. She does look amazing though. Did I just call her Princess in a good way?

"Thanks cowboy but can we get back to business." She says hastily making me think my reaction made her a little happy. Maybe she did the transformation for my benefit. Nah couldn't be. She hates me. I freeze when the thought of another man crosses my mind. Maybe she did this for him. I don't like that idea at all. I'll have to ask Aiden to find out if there is another guy in Leah's life now.

## 18

As we're nearing the end of the storm preparations, the rain starts to come down in sheets. I have never seen it rain this hard in my life. Before we could realize just how bad, the creek starts to rise on the line between town and the nursery. It's now completely covering the bridge at the entrance to the nursery. Meaning we have no way of getting out in a vehicle. Wonderful. I guess I can just swim to the other side and walk home.

"I'm going to walk home." I tell Austin while rolling up my pant legs and sleeves. "You going to stay here?"

"You aren't walking anywhere Leah. The current will take you with it. You will never get out of that creek alive." He says knowing that he is stuck with me.

"But I can't stay here Austin. I have to get home. There is nowhere but the office to stay and there are two of us." I shriek knowing I can't stay with him.

"Leah, the couch in there makes into a bed and I will take the floor. No worries. We will be safer here and by daylight the water levels will be down and we can go home." He says walking towards the back room.

"Are you sure? We might kill each other before daybreak." I say knowing full well I can't keep a smile off my face. Until he smiles right back and my stomach gets butterflies. What are we in for?

"Yes Leah I'm sure. I won't kill you, I promise."

Maybe this will all work out. Maybe he and I can get along for the sake of the nursery. That creek had better go down because I want to go home as soon as possible. Close quarters with Austin Blake is not a good idea. At all. Especially when he's standing there with a tight t-shirt and faded blue jeans on. Holy cow.

*******************

"What else do we need to do? Do you guys have storms like this often?"

"No, it's pretty rare that we get a storm like this. We still need to put sandbags in front of each door that leads outside and in front of all the potting shed doors. They're raised up so they won't get water directly in them, but when the creek rises like this we are better safe than sorry."

"Where are the sandbags? Is that what that pile of white pillow looking stuff is in the warehouse?"

"Yes Leah those are sandbags. Not white pillows." I say laughing and turning away to head to the warehouse. She is such a city girl. White pillow looking stuff. You would think they have sand bags in New York but I guess not.

"You can quit shaking your head and laughing at me mister."

"It's tough not to when you call them that. It's not every day I hear them called white pillow looking things."

"Sorry, I didn't know what they were. We lived on the 14th floor of our building growing up so I never had to worry about flooding."

"I didn't mean to make fun, just caught me off guard. Help me carry these to the front door."

We keep busy for the next hour and a half carrying sandbags to the front, side and back doors of the nursery itself. I know we have the outside potting sheds still to do but Leah looks exhausted.

"You look beat. How about you go in the office and shut down the computer and electronics in there and I'll take the rest of these out to the potting sheds."

"Okay I can do that. I guess being a girl from New York isn't cut out for carrying tons of sandbags. Sorry. I guess I need to work out if I have to get used to this. I'll be in the office if you need me."

*******************

I turn to walk to the office when I get a thought in my head and turn to ask Austin a question. But before I can get anything spit out I freeze at the sight before me. Austin is bent down picking up sandbags and slinging them onto his shoulder. The muscles in his legs and arms are bulging with all the strain. Oh my goodness. He is so beautiful. He could be a male goddess and no one else seems to see that in this small town? They could have the next underwear model underneath their noses and are oblivious. Goodness he is so hot. As I am picturing this strong man in his underwear posing for cameras, he turns around and catches me mid-dream.

"Enjoying the view?"

"Um, no. Yes. Wait what are you talking about?" I lie knowing exactly what he just caught me doing. He caught me with that look of lust on my face. Wonderful.

"Nothing. Did you need something?"

"Ah, no I forgot what I was going to ask. See you in a bit." And with that I high tail it out of there as quick as I can. How embarrassing. That man just caught me ogling him like a piece of meat.

What is happening to me? Stomping back to the office I continue to have an inner battle with my hormones. This man makes me feels things that I do not want to feel. Things I haven't felt for years. Things that I know are dangerous for me to feel.

## 19

She was checking me out. She was seriously just checking me out. Hmmm. She didn't look too excited to be caught though. This might be a long night. I don't understand why she is ashamed to be attracted to me. Maybe that is why she doesn't like me. Maybe I make her feels things she doesn't want to feel. But why?

I have a few hours to change her mind about me. How do I do that? I think she feels the same way I do but how do I know for sure? Karlie. I'll call Karlie.

Stepping into one of the potting sheds so that Leah can't overhear my conversation I dial my sister in law's number.

"Hey Karlie, what's up?"

"Hi Austin, not much. Are you done prepping for the storm? Is everything ok?"

"Yes, everything is fine. We are about done I just needed to ask you a serious question."

"Ok, shoot."

"It doesn't go any farther than us, got it?"

"Um, let me guess this has to do with Leah and how she feels about you. Am I right?"

"How do you women do that?"

"I don't know we just do. You like her don't you?"

"Yes. A lot more than I ever wanted to. The more time I spend with her the more I find myself thinking about her and wanting to talk to her."

"Understandable. She is a great person Austin. You couldn't have picked a better woman to fall in love with if you ask me."

"Fall in love with? Whoa not so fast. I am not in love with her, just attracted to her."

"Whatever you say. What are you calling me for then?"

"I was hoping you could tell me how she feels about me. I don't want to try to get closer to her if she isn't into me. Do you think she feels the same as I do?"

"Austin. Why would I tell you that? That is breaking girl code and you know I would never tell you something that she has told me in confidence."

"You just did thanks Karlie."

"No I didn't! Damn you Austin! How do you men always get us women to tell you whatever you want? Whatever you do, don't tell her I told you that!!"

"I won't I promise. And Karlie, I LOVE YOU!! My brother is one lucky man!"

"Ya ya ya. Go get the girl you jerk!"

Laughing, I hang up my phone and finish preparing the potting sheds before walking back inside the nursery and towards the office where I know Leah is. I picture her sitting with her head lying in one hand that is propped up on the desk and reading the screen with squinted eyes like she always does. She has a scowl on her face the whole time like its Greek she's reading. I guess this is all Greek to her since she's been a model her whole life. Have I been too hard on her? That changes right now.

\*\*\*\*\*\*\*\*\*\*\*\*\*\*\*\*\*\*\*

"Did you get it all shut down?" I hear from the doorway of the office. I should have had it all done yes, but I have been a little preoccupied with the vision of Austin out there that I saw. And him busting me doing it.

"Um ya except the computer. I was checking on the weather radar. It looks like quite a storm we are getting and the worst part isn't even here yet. You think those sandbags are going to work?"

"Hope so. That's all we can do. We need to get that shut off soon in case we get some bad lightening. Wouldn't want to fry that system. We don't need the expense to replace it all."

"Got it. All shut down. Now what do we do?"

"We wait it out. Once the creek goes down and the bridge is uncovered, we can go home. That might be awhile though."

"Hmmm well do we have any cards around here?"

"Yes actually Jack and I played cards one of his last good days here. Let me see if I can find them. I believe they might be in that upper right drawer."

Austin walks to my left side and reaches across me and opens the drawer to my right. My body is more than aware that he is close. Very close. I don't dare look up at him; he has seen me checking him out enough for a lifetime.

"Leah, look at me. I'm not going to bite you." I hear him say as he gets the cards and returns to his spot across from the desk from me. A much safer place for him to be. It's going to be a long night if we are stuck in this small office alone.

"What? I didn't think you were going to. Ready to play? What's your specialty?"

"Poker."

"Really? I love poker. Grandpa taught me how to play years ago. I haven't played for a while though so bear with me. What are we playing for?"

"Let's make it interesting."

"What did you have in mind?"

"Strip poker."

"You're kidding. I thought you were going to say something like my car or the nursery ownership. But strip poker? Why?"

"Just sounds fun. I don't want your car and I am okay with the ownership right now. Are you scared to play strip poker?"

"I am far from scared. Just surprised."

"Winner with the most clothes on after five rounds wins. Then we will start all over if we need to."

"You deal. I'm ready. Get ready to strip cowboy."

"Oh Princess don't be so confident. I am really good at this game."

"We shall see." I say not able to control the big grin spreading across my face. I didn't tell Austin the whole truth. Lewis and I had weekly poker parties with his baseball friends. I am pretty good. I kinda hope Austin isn't very good. What I wouldn't do to see him in nothing but his undies. That modeling gig in his underwear vision hits me again. I feel my face heat with the realization that I might actually see Austin strip down or oh my goodness he could see me stripped down. I immediately try to remember which bra and panties

I wore today hoping they match and that they aren't old and tattered.

Luckily I wore a good set today. I think.

## 20

"Alright Princess you weren't exactly honest about your poker abilities. I have lost my shoes and socks. Next is my shirt while you sit there fully clothed. What gives?"

"I told you I learned when I was younger and hadn't played for a while. I didn't say how long awhile is. You were the cocky one. Not feeling so cocky now?"

"I'll turn up the heat. I was trying to be nice but no more Mr. Nice Guy. Game on."

"Let's go. You have to take off your pants or shirt next."

After a few more hands she has her shoes and socks off too. One more hand and I will either see her without a shirt or pants. My body can't seem to think of anything but what she will look like either way.

"Ok Princess, read 'em and weep. Full house."

"Damn! I thought I had you!"

"Pants or shirt? Your choice."

"Um, pants." And she stands up starting to unbutton her jeans. The anticipation is killing me.

She slowly slips them down her legs and steps out of them. I can't seem to feel my hands. I want so badly to reach over and feel those toned legs that look like they are softer than silk. She has the most gorgeous legs I have ever seen. How do I play any more hands of poker when all I can see is her stripping off those jeans and them hitting the floor?

\*\*\*\*\*\*\*\*\*\*\*\*\*\*\*\*\*\*\*

I can't believe I just took my jeans off in front of Austin. Oh my goodness. He looked like he had seen a ghost though. Could he really think I am attractive? I have got to win the next two hands before I sit here without a shirt too. I would love more than anything right now to see him without his shirt.

"Next hand you lose your shirt cowboy."

"We shall see Princess."

These cards were the best hand yet, a royal flush. I have him this time. From the look on his face he doesn't have anything close to that.

"I think I get your shirt. Whatcha got?"

"Damn! Not that good! How did you do that?"

"Maybe you were a bit distracted? The storm is pretty loud out there."

"The storm yes that's what had me distracted. Fine, my shirt as you requested."

As he rips his shirt over his head I about choke on my tongue. My heart leaps up into my throat. Holy crap this man is amazing. Amazing. What it would be like to touch him. To run my hands down his chest. Or feel those strong arms around me. Whoa girl chill out. Deep breath.

"Ok, last hand. Either you lose your pants or I lose my shirt. Ready?"

"You have no idea how ready Princess."

Just as I start dealing out the cards, thunder hits so loudly that I jump and throw the cards everywhere. I jump out of my chair and come out from around the desk and turn around to face behind me where it sounded like the thunder came from. Of course Austin is there to catch me once I turn around.

Those strong arms are around me. Am I dreaming? How can this be happening?

"Um, sorry about that. That was so loud it scared the crap out of me. Sorry."

"I think we are done playing aren't we?"

"Yes. I can't sit there anymore. That really has my heart racing. Scared me so badly. The thunder here sounds like it's outside the windows. We never had storms this bad in New York. This is crazy."

"Let's go sit out back under the awning in the warehouse. It always smells so good when it's raining too."

"Ok that sounds awesome. But I do want my pants before we do that. And here's your shirt cowboy. I would say we're even."

I say that and he smiles while he shrugs his t-shirt back on. I am a little saddened to see him cover that magnificence up. But I would have trouble making complete sentences if he kept it off. Much better idea. I do have to work with this man tomorrow. Tomorrow seems like forever away though.

"You got off easy. You were losing that shirt the next round Princess."

"Keep telling yourself that cowboy." And I walk away towards the warehouse. I have to get out of that room. It's too close quarters for all that flirting. Flirting? Were we really flirting? Could he really feel the same? Oh boy.

## 21

Karlie wasn't lying when she told me Leah felt the same about me. Okay maybe she pretty much said it but not the exact words. She was flirting with me right back. The look on her face when she realized I had taken her in my arms after the thunder told me all I needed to know. She was fighting the urge to kiss me. That's why she pushed out of my arms so quickly.

"Doesn't this smell great? Best part of storms here. I have always loved them since I was a kid. I would sit in the barn and listen to the rain and smell this wonderful smell."

"It does smell great. What was it like growing up here?"

"It was great. Everyone around here knows you and is always willing to help out any way they can. It's kinda like an extension of your family."

"You mean nosey and want to know what everyone else is doing?"

"Yes, that might be part of it but they would drop anything to help if you needed it."

"True. Well, it would have been very different than New York. There you only knew a few people in your class and in our building I knew the door man better than I knew my next door neighbor."

"So like in the movies eh? Raised by the building workers?"

"Not quite smarty pants. Dad was there just busy. When you see a certain person every time you go in and out of your house you get to know them. They saw me grow up and I got to know them too. Knew how many kids they had and such. It was like an extension of my family like you said."

"Interesting. What are you doing here then?"

"I needed a new start."

"A new start? What does that mean?"

"Austin I would rather not talk about it right now."

After sitting outside for about an hour I hear her stomach growl and realize that I am a bit hungry too.

"Hey let's go heat up the leftovers Mom sent with me today."

"I take it you heard my stomach huh?"

"Yes, thought I better feed you before you eat me."

"We haven't been stranded that long.  No cannibalism yet."

**\*\*\*\*\*\*\*\*\*\*\*\*\*\*\*\*\*\***

"So, do you miss New York?" I ask her while putting the dishes in the microwave.  Glad I listened to mom and took the leftovers from lunch with me this afternoon.

"Not really.  Like I told you before, genuinely I love it here. Wouldn't you miss Colvin if you left?" she asks while blowing on her dinner.

"I went to college in Denver but came back as soon as I could.  I missed the wide open spaces and my family." I say knowing she didn't have much family. "Were you and your parents close growing up?"

"Yes and no.  Mom died from breast cancer when I was in middle school and Dad threw himself into work to hide his pain of losing her.  All the while he still had me around and I knew he loved me; he was just always very busy.  That's why when I met- never mind." She says then stops short. "What did you study in Denver?"

"What were you going to say? When you met your husband? You can tell me Leah I won't judge. I am over that I promise."

"You don't want to know the whole story, believe me." She says quickly trying to move away. "No one wants to know that story."

"Leah I want to get to know you. I like you and we are business partners whether we like it or not. I want to know more. Please trust me and tell me." I plead wanting to know anything I could about this beautiful and complex woman in front of me waiting out the storm. I am almost thankful for this storm now.

## 22

I can't believe I told Austin the whole story tonight. Well, not the whole story. Not about Shannon. I have never told anyone the entire story. Austin sat there with concern written all over his face but never asked questions. He let me get it all out. When I started to cry, he just handed me a Kleenex and waited for me to finish.

After the storm let up early in the night we went our separate ways feeling a little better about our relationship. If that's what you call it. Friendship? What were we anyway? Business partners? Yes, business partners.

As I get ready for bed I scrub my face, brush my hair and put on my tee shirt that I like to wear to bed. Leaving my feet bare and just panties on under, I crawl into bed thinking about Austin and the way he acted when I confided in him. He was so gentle and acted like he was really concerned for me. He is definitely nothing like Lewis.

I startle when I hear noises that sound like someone outside the house.

Knock. Knock. Knock.

I hear it again and start down the stairs towards the front door. I can see through the glass of the door that it's Austin. What in the world is he doing here so late at night? I hope nothing happened to the nursery.

"Austin, is something wrong with the nursery?" I say whipping the door open as quickly as I could, forgetting how I'm dressed.

"No Leah its fine. I'm not really sure what I'm doing here. I just couldn't go home." He says slowly. "I couldn't get you out of my head."

"Austin, what are you saying?" I can't believe what I'm hearing.

"Leah, I want you. It took all the strength I had not to wrap my arms around you tonight when you were telling me about your past. I wanted to pull you to me and feel your body against mine." He chokes out not letting his eyes leave mine. "I wanted to let you know that you're safe now."

Before I can reply he grabs my arms and pulls me to him. He wraps his arms around me and I look up at his face in shock. I can clearly see the desire and need in his eyes. He begins to drop his lips to mine and I suck in a breath when our lips meet. He starts the kiss gentle and sweet but eventually it turns heated and passionate.

I have never in my life been kissed like that. Never felt such sparks and swirls in my stomach like I do when I am with Austin. I definitely haven't felt this wanted by a man. Even my ex-husband.

I run my hands up his chest and down. I slip my hands under his shirt to feel his hard and hot chest. The moment I touch him I feel on fire. He runs his hands down my back and over my bottom. He pulls me closer to him where I fit against his hard length. I can easily feel how much he wants me. If his passionate kisses didn't tell me then his erection gives it away. He runs his hands up my back under my t-shirt and my skin sizzles with his touch.

I wind my arms around his neck and in his hair. He smells so heavenly and all male. I want to make love to this man more than I have wanted anything in my whole life. I hear myself moan as his tongue touches just below my ear. I move against him and hear his growl from deep inside his throat.

"Where is your bedroom Leah?" he says breathlessly between kisses. I look up and realize that we are still standing with the front door wide open.

Shutting the door, I take his hand and lead him to my room. Not yet able to use the master where my grandparents had slept, I begin to feel awkward about being with him in my childhood room. He must have felt me hesitate and he pulls away and kisses my shoulder.

"Are you not sure about this Leah?" he asks looking deep in my eyes. "We can stop now if you aren't. I won't make you do anything you don't want to do."

"No Austin, I want you to make love to me, I just don't know about doing so in my childhood bedroom." I say starting to feel shy.

"Honey I don't care where it is we make love, I just have to do it now. I am burning up for you." He says as he picks me up and carries me the rest of the way down the hall to my room.

\*\*\*\*\*\*\*\*\*\*\*\*\*\*\*\*\*\*

"I think the pink curtains set the mood." I say once I know she is awake with a big smile and kiss her shoulder.

"They are awful. But you were amazing. Last night was the best night of my life."

"And morning. Don't forget this morning." I say smiling so wide it hurts. "What do you want for breakfast?"

"I want a shower first then we can go see what there is. Probably not much since I don't cook." She says shyly.

"We can go to Sally's if you are up for being seen with me." I say before kissing her shoulder again.

"I think that would be great. Meet in the shower in five?" she says as she kisses me soundly on the lips and leaves with an ornery grin on her face that makes me smile even wider.

"You don't have to ask me twice!" I say watching her run to the bathroom naked and beautiful. Could this really be happening? I just sigh and run after her.

## 23

"What can I get you two? It's about time you decided to quit being mad at each other." Sally says as she winks at Austin and me.

"We just came in for breakfast before going to the nursery Sally." I say quickly while looking at the menu. I see nothing but blurred words as I wish she would go away.

"You too are holding hands and smiling. Looks to me like it's more than that. Finally. The whole town has been counting down the days 'til you two fell in love." Sally says matter of factly.

"Sally I will have the special." I say trying not to look at Austin.

"Same for me." He finally says and she leaves the table.

"I'm sorry about that Austin." I say sheepishly. "If you want to take it to go I won't mind."

"Princess I could care less that everyone sees me happy and with you. Doesn't bother me in the least." He says smiling. "Unless you're embarrassed to be seen with me."

"No Austin I'm not. I just don't want to put the cart before the horse. I like you and I loved being with you last night and this morning." I say trying to convey my feelings through those words and see him smile at the morning part.

"Good, then it's settled." He says as he gets up and sits next to me and puts his arm around me and pulls me in for a kiss. A kiss that showed everyone in the place just how close we were now. A kiss that made me want to rip his clothes off right here in the middle of the café.

"Well, you two sure look cozy." We hear a woman say beside Austin.

We both look up to see Amelia standing at the end of our table smiling that huge Blake smile.

"Hi Mom. You remember Leah don't you?" Austin says.

"Of course I remember her. Can I sit down?" she asks looking at me.

"You are more than welcome to." I say quickly averting my gaze to see if the food is coming to change the subject. How embarrassing. His mother seeing us making out like teenagers in public.

"You don't need to be embarrassed Leah. AJ and I were the same way once we got over being mad at each other too. He was a man that I was supposed to hate because his family hated my roommate's family but things didn't quite happen that way." Amelia said smiling as she reminisced.

"Mom we don't need the details. I think she gets it. You're happy for us. Right?" Austin says looking from his mom to me.

"Yes dear. As soon as I met Leah I knew she was the one for you." Amelia says as she gets up. "I just hope I didn't scare you away from my son dear. We are having a family dinner at the 6AB tomorrow night. Please say you will come with him Leah."

"Bye mom." Austin said standing up to give her a hug goodbye. She winked at me and I waved.

"Well, that went well I think. Do you wanna go with me to the dinner?" he says once he sits back down beside me.

"Austin I would do just about anything you asked me to do." I say smiling and knowing that my heart is finally on the mend. All because of some dumb cocky cowboy. Who would have thought? Grandpa, that's who. I'm sure he is happier than ever up there in Heaven watching his matchmaking come together.

## 24

"Are you sure you wanna do this? They can be a lot to handle."

"Yes I'm sure. I've never really been around a big family so I'm kinda excited."

"Ok, just remember you said that." I say to Leah as we get out of my pickup at my parents' house on the 6AB.

"Let's go chicken. They can't be that bad." She grabs my hand and heads for the front door.

Walking into the house with Leah seems so much different than it has felt before. I grew up in this house and have walked in the door a million times, but it has never felt as good as it does now. The house itself feels different, almost more like a home. Which is weird because it was a wonderful home growing up. I just can't explain it.

"Austin I am so glad you came and brought Leah with you."

"Mom I always come when you ask me to."

"Ok maybe I am just excited that you brought a woman with you this time."

"Thanks a lot Mom that makes me sound like I haven't had a date in years."

"Have you? If you have you haven't brought her around here."

"Ok let's move on Leah. Don't listen to my mother and her babbling she isn't helping my case."

"Would you like any help in the kitchen Amelia? I would be more than happy to help."

Mom winks at me and says directly to Leah, "That would be great Leah. Audrey and Karlie are in there already so just follow me. She will see you later at dinner Son."

"Be nice Mom."

"Of course I will be nice. I happen to really like this girl. So just go hang out with the guys and I will return her to you at dinner."

"Wow so much love Mom. Leah I'll be in here if you need me. Don't let them bite."

"I will be fine, just go." She smiles that big smile that melts my insides. I am going to fall for this girl faster than I ever have before. And from the looks of it my mother couldn't be happier about that.

*******************

"Leah, hi! I'm so glad you could make it!" Karlie squeals and wraps me in a big hug, well as big as she can get with her belly. Maybe Aiden was right and it did double in size over night. Poor girl.

"I know, it's huge. Don't remind me."

"I didn't say a word."

"You didn't have to. Everyone looks at my belly and gets that same look on their face."

"Sorry, you look beautiful and glowing if that helps."

"Ya ya ya, just stir these noodles please, it's too hot standing by the stove for me."

"What are we making?"

"Chicken and noodles with mashed potatoes and fresh green beans straight from Amelia's garden. She is very proud of them."

"They look yummy. It's been awhile since I have had a real home cooked meal. At least one that isn't from Sally's. I'm sure Ramen and toast don't count."

"Oh goodness Leah, you come out here and I will cook for you anytime you want. I will make sure Austin knows to bring you more often. He eats here almost every day, well whenever he can get away from the nursery."

"I am hoping things are slowing down there for him now that I am getting a better handle on things. He won't be pulled in so many different directions."

"He isn't complaining. He loves that place. And I think he kinda likes the company he keeps there too." I see Amelia and Karlie share mischievous grins. They are definitely in this matchmaking together. Good thing Austin and I are ok with that now.

"This dinner has to be better than the one I had at my house Leah. You two could have stabbed each other with your forks."

"Oh don't remind me. That was terrible. I acted like such a child."

"You weren't the only one from what I hear. Now let's finish this up and feed those starving men out there. And Karlie before she eats straight out of the pots." Amelia says from behind me as she takes bread out of the oven.

I smile and feel the warmth inside me as I look around at how great this place and this family is. I could get used to this kindness and love. But can I really allow myself to fall for Austin? If I haven't already.

## 25

"So, Son I hear you brought Miss Stampley with you tonight? I take it things are getting better at the nursery?"

"Dad, her name is Leah and yes we are trying to get along."

"Along? That's what they call it these days?"

"Austin you know Dad knows more than you think he does. Mom told him she saw you two yesterday in Sally's making out like teenagers. You might as well spill."

"There's nothing to spill. We just started getting to know each other a little better in the past couple of days and might actually like each other instead of despise each other."

"Despise? You two couldn't even sit at our dining table that night we had you both over without shooting dirty looks at the other."

"I know that was terrible. We acted like children. I'm sorry for that."

"Well I sure hope you two can get along while sitting at your Mom & I's dining table tonight."

"Yes sir we can. That I can promise."

"By the size of that smile on your face I can only imagine why you can make that kind of a promise Son."

"Are you still wanting to buy her ownership out and send her on her merry way back to New York?" My Dad always knows how to ask the hard questions.

"I really don't know right now Dad. If you would have asked me that two days ago I would still have told you yes, but since Leah and I have been getting along so well and really hitting it off, I'm not so sure."

"So you think that Jack knew what he was doing after all splitting the ownership like he did?"

"I'm beginning to wonder. He's doing a fine job of matchmaking from Heaven that's for sure. I'm sure the storm was his handiwork knowing we would get stranded there together and would have to talk."

"Are you complaining?"

"Not in the least." I smile and remember the way Leah looked when she was slipping those jeans off during our game of poker. That girl gets my motor revving that is for sure.

"Earth to Austin. Do I want to know what you are day dreaming about with that goofy smile on your face? You used to have that smile when your Mom would tell you that Jack's granddaughter was in town. And I can bet it's about that same girl." Dad says and slaps me on the back and walks out of the study leaving me to remember those days. Happily.

\*\*\*\*\*\*\*\*\*\*\*\*\*\*\*\*\*\*\*

"Hey, I see you survived the kitchen trio." Austin says as I walk towards him in the dining room. He has a slight smile on his face that tells me he has been thinking about something important. But do I even want to ask?

"Of course I did. They are amazing women. You are very lucky to have them in your life Austin."

"I am, believe me. About as much as I am to have you in my life." He says and plants a sweet kiss on my lips. We both know this kiss can't ignite anything right now so it lasts only a second. But of course it's enough to get the sparks flying all over again. Even in the middle of Austin's family's dining room.

"Ok you two, we're all starving." Aiden says from behind us. Great, made a spectacle of ourselves. I can feel the heat creeping up my neck and into my face. That is very embarrassing. I just met most of these people. But when I look up at Austin he has a look of pride on his face as he smiles and squeezes my hand before pulling out my chair. After sitting down I realize that I'm seated next to Karlie. Thank God for small miracles. I don't know what I would do if I was seated by any of Austin's other family members.

"Sorry about that." I hear him whisper into my ear and the vibration from his words on my ear gives me goose bumps all over. This man knows just what he does to me. I have to admit that I love every minute of it.

After Austin sits down I look over at him and he's got this mischievous look on his face telling me that he has something up his sleeve. But I decide it's my turn to get him. I reach over and put my hand high on his thigh and rub slowly towards his knee. He had just taken a drink of his iced tea and chokes almost spitting it out. Score one for Leah! Now I am getting the look that I had better watch out. Retaliation. At least no one else here knew what just happened.

That is until I look across the table at Audrey and she is smiling and trying to hide it. Great, I wasn't successful in my covert plan. What she must think of me. Oh well, Austin liked it. Smiling I decide I had better keep my hands and eyes to myself or I will never get through this meal. And that's a good thing because his family likes to talk during meals. A lot.

*******************

"Thank you so much for inviting me. It was so delicious." Leah says to my Mom while giving her a hug goodbye. Mom is hearing wedding bells already I'm sure. She just smiles at me and leaves the room once Dad does the same.

"I will call you later." Aiden tells me and I see Karlie whispering into Leah's ear causing a slight red tint to come over her. I can only imagine what that is about. Just to make things even more interesting, I walk over to Leah and put my arm around her waist and pull her closer to my side. Good grief I love the feel of her there. She feels so natural. Do I really believe that she was made to be by my side?

"Ready to go?"

"Yep, if you are."

"Yep, I can't wait to get you home. Your place or mine?"

"You can take me home then you can go to yours."

"Ahhhhhh really? I was hoping I could stay again tonight with you. Maybe not get much sleep."

"I really do need some sleep Austin. I will meet you for breakfast in the morning at Sally's."

"Ugh I did not see that answer coming. I guess if that's what you want. I can walk you to the door though right?"

"Of course. What kind of a date would this be?" At least she holds my hand all the way back to town.

Pulling up in front of Leah's house makes me start to regret her answer even more. I want nothing more than to make love to this woman all night long. I could really get used to that every night. And every morning. Whoa, moving a little fast there. Maybe I'm scaring her off.

Getting out of the pickup to walk her to the door makes me feel like a teenager again. Wanting more but only able to give a good night kiss then leave wanting much more.

## 26

Sleeping in this house is strange now. After spending nights at Leah's, this house isn't a home anymore. Almost like someone else lives here and I'm just visiting. Even after being away from the 6AB for four years it still feels like home when I'm there, so what's going on? I don't understand this. How could I get so attached and comfortable being with Leah at her house so quickly? Of course I'm not able to sleep without her body pressed up against mine. Not being able to smell her or feel her is getting to me. I just saw her a few hours ago but I miss her terribly. How has this little red headed thing gotten under my skin so deeply? There's an ache inside me that is gnawing at me and driving me insane. I pray she isn't having the same fate that I am.

I toss and turn for another hour and decide it's time to get up. I walk down the hallway to my kitchen and see that the light is on. It's three in the morning; I don't remember leaving it on last night. The further I go I see that someone's moving inside the room. Who in the world would be in here so early?

"Aiden, what in the heck are you doing in my kitchen at this hour?"

"Hey man. Sorry, Karlie got mad at me so I left. She was very upset about something stupid and I don't think I helped much with my comments. I guess it's the hormones."

"Can't handle the lady already? How are you going to do it when the baby comes? You can't just run away at the first sign of trouble."

"Duh. She was very upset and I didn't want to go to the 6AB and have Mom all over the situation. Karlie will be fine in the morning. I just needed somewhere to crash. I didn't think you would be here anyway. Why aren't you at Leah's? Trouble in your paradise?"

"Shut it. I'm not really sure why she wanted to be alone but she did. Once we got home from dinner she told me to drop her off. I guess you guys were too much for her in one night."

"Doubtful. She probably figured out what a dud you are!"

"Why are you in my kitchen at three am?"

"Ha ha. Now do you want some breakfast too? What are you doing awake Romeo?"

"If you're making it, sure. I couldn't sleep. Just tossing and turning. I'm supposed to meet Leah at Sally's at 7 but a little now shouldn't hurt. Thanks brother. I'm sure Karlie will love you again by morning."

"Ya, she just needed a breather I guess. She has been getting crankier and crankier as this pregnancy goes on. Going to be a long couple of months."

"Glad it's you and not me."

"Ya you have enough issues with keeping your woman happy. Do I need to give you a few pointers?"

"Shut up and eat you knucklehead or I'll call Karlie and tell her what you said about her being cranky."

"You wouldn't dare."

Laughing, I sit down to enjoy my brother's eggs. He could probably tell me just how to handle this with Leah but I don't understand it myself. Maybe Aiden is right and she did figure out that I'm not as good of a catch as she first thought.

\* \* \* \* \* \* \* \* \* \* \* \* \* \* \* \* \* \*

Last night without Austin beside me was miserable. I miss him like I would miss my coffee in the morning. Maybe more. I smile at that thought knowing I LOVE my coffee. Of course I didn't get much sleep and had too much time to ponder my growing concern of the seriousness of this thing he and I have going. I don't want another relationship but I really like being around Austin besides just at the nursery. Is it selfish not to want commitment? I sound like a guy and what every woman in America complains about. I am really screwed up. If I fall for Austin or let him in like I did with Lewis, I'll be vulnerable to get hurt again. I DO NOT want to be hurt again like that. I'm not sure I can survive. And if I let him get closer to me, I would have to tell him the whole truth about that night. Ugh.

The time we spend together is so good though and it makes me ache for something more. Just being around Austin makes me want to come home after a hard day and spend time with him. To be able to cook dinner and watch a movie with him, just being with him feels so natural and easy. But then my head gets involved in this argument and it says NO! Which to listen to? Which will keep me happy? Which will keep me from getting hurt? Of course they are not the same! Why can't life ever be easy? IS that too much to ask for? Grrrrr!

Getting out of bed I drag myself into the shower. A good long and hot shower should wake me up and ease the tension in my muscles. As I let the water run over my head and down my body, I remember how wonderful the Blake family was to me last night and how hard it was to keep the feelings at bay. It would be so easy to fall into the rhythm of being a part of their family. But I just can't do that yet. I would be so happy and love being there and then a cold sweat would overcome me and I felt like I was going to pass out. I don't think anyone noticed, but I couldn't let Austin see me break down after I got home. I knew I was walking on thin ice with the emotions when we were saying our goodbyes and everyone was so nice and welcoming to me. I wanted nothing more than to have him come home with me again but knew I had had too much and needed space. Maybe didn't want it but needed it. I can only hope he understands. But how can he if I can't explain it to him? Grrrrr!

After my torturous shower, I'm dressed and almost ready. I look in the mirror to make sure my hair and makeup is good and as I do I don't recognize myself. Gone are the bruises and sadness. I actually look good and happy. This is shocking to me after all I have been through these past few months. A wave of relief rushes over me as I decide it's time to try this thing I have with Austin. He is the most wonderful man I have ever met. I can't let him get away. No matter how scared I am.

With a new sense of relief, I walk out my door and to my car. I am going to meet Austin and just might fall in love with this man. If I haven't already.

I swallow the doubt that tries to creep up and I breathe in deep. Just keep walking Leah, just keep walking. Austin is waiting. For me.

## 27

She's late. Maybe five more minutes. If she doesn't show up this morning for breakfast, what does that mean? Does it mean she hates me again? Good grief I can't go back to being unfriendly with this woman. That was terrible. Especially not after we have gotten as close as two bodies can get. Heck especially not since I think I'm falling in love with her. How can that be? Already? All I know is that I can't imagine being without her.

"You look deep in thought Austin. Whatcha thinkin about?"

"There you are. I was wondering if you were standing me up."

"Nope. I kinda overslept. Just a little." I stand up and motion for her to sit. I think she might sit on the opposite side of the booth from me but she rises up and kisses me first then slips in where I was sitting. Nice. That's where I would have preferred.

"So, have you already ordered?"

"Nah, I was waiting on you. Do you know what you want?"

"Blueberry pancakes please. Just water to drink." She smiles up at me and melts all the fears and uneasiness I had been struggling with. She does like me still. That's a big relief. I can rest easy and enjoy my breakfast.

"Did you sleep well?"

"No. That's why I overslept. You?"

"Can I get you crazy kids something to eat?"

"Hey Sally. Blueberry pancakes for the lady and I will have my normal. Thank you."

"It really is good to see you two together. Your grandpa used to tell us all the time that he knew you two were going to be together someday."

"Wow. How long ago was that? I quit coming here many years ago."

"He said it every day until he couldn't make it in anymore. He thought very highly of Mr. Austin sitting here. He's a good one, make sure you keep him. I'll be right back with your breakfast."

"Well, Mr. Austin here was quite fond of the man himself." I say and smile at Leah. "And I am all for his prediction."

"Grandpa loved you as much as he loved the rest of us. I guess he knew something good when he saw it too." She wraps her arms around my one arm and hugs me tight from the side. She feels so good being this close.

"You see something good here in Colvin?" I ask hoping to not sound too desperate for a yes answer.

"I see quite a few good things here. I plan on staying. Can you handle that?"

"If that means you will be here with me, I can handle anything." I put my arm around her and pull her closer kissing her cheek. This woman is under my skin. Way under.

"You know Leah; this is the same thing you always ordered when you would come in with your grandparents. Nice to see that some things never change." Sally says as she brings out our food.

"That's so weird because I have never liked them anywhere but here. I have even tried making them myself and they never taste right."

"Well you let me know if these do the trick or not."

"I will. I'm sure they're perfect. Thank you."

"You two enjoy your meal." She winks at me and I can't help but smile. Life couldn't be more perfect right now.

After we devour our food and talk about everything under the sun, we are both ready to go to work. At our nursery. That sounds so good. Funny how I hated the thought of that a while back when Roget broke the news, but now I kinda like the idea. I could handle working side by side with Leah the rest of our lives. Wow, I am talking forever. Whoa boy.

"Ready to go boss?"

"Austin, I am not your boss and you know it."

"Ok, are you ready to go partner? We have a big load coming in this morning."

"Yep, meet you there partner." And she gives me a big kiss that might have lasted a bit longer than it should have since we are standing in the middle of a public sidewalk.

## 28

"Hey Karlie, what's up?"

"Leah, do you want to go to Tulsa with me to get some of the baby's things? I have a few things I can't find here and I need a break from all things Blake."

"I would love to. When were you wanting to go?"

"How about tomorrow? Are you working at the nursery?"

"No we decided to close it down with it being Saturday and he wanted to help his parents at the cabin."

"Perfect. I'll pick you up at eight."

"I'll be ready. See you then!" I hang up my cell phone and throw it on my bed with a large sigh.

Great. Spending a whole day with a pregnant Karlie shopping for a baby. A baby. How am I going to survive this? It's going to be tough for sure. What was I thinking?

"Austin, I guess I'm going with Karlie tomorrow to Tulsa baby shopping."

"That should be fun. But I take it from the look on your face you aren't excited?"

How do I say this? "Not at all." I finally say and think that maybe that wasn't the right wording.

"Why? I think it would be fun looking at all the little person things."

"Sure if you say so."

"I don't understand why you aren't happy about going but if you are this miserable just call Karlie back and tell her you can't go."

"I can't. There's no one else to go and I already agreed to go."

"What's wrong?"

"Nothing. Just tired and grumpy. I'll get over it."

"Leah, talk to me."

"It's nothing. I'm going to take a hot bath. Been a long day and my body hurts from that last shipment we unloaded."

"Enjoy your bath. I'll go home tonight and let you sleep without waking you up. It's gonna be late when I get home from the 6AB."

"You really don't have to. I sleep better when you're here next to me."

"You sure? It really is going to be late. Probably around midnight."

"Yes, come back." I slip my arms around his neck and lightly touch my lips to his. Those lips that seem to make everything right in the world. As he walks away I wonder why it is that I can't seem to tell him about my baby. He needs to know and would understand a lot more about me if he did. Will it ever feel right to tell anyone though?

I walk to the bathtub and slip out of my clothes. I step into the water and sigh loudly as I sink lower and lower feeling the stress of the day soak away. Just what I needed.

## 29

"What time are you leaving this morning?" I say rubbing her bare leg that's draped over mine. I've been lying here listening to her breathe for the past hour. She seems so peaceful after being upset about today's shopping trip.

"Never if you don't stop doing that."

"Do you want me to stop doing this? Or this?" I say kissing her neck then her collarbone. I can feel her breathing getting faster and faster the more I kiss her anywhere but the lips. She tries to turn her head for me to connect with them but I lift my head up at the last moment and kiss her nose getting a grunt in response.

"I could skip it if you kiss my lips this time."

"Karlie would be so disappointed to lose her shopping buddy. Seriously, what time is she picking you up?"

"She said eight, I think. But that was before you were kissing me. Don't really remember anything right now."

"Well, we have a little bit of time before then. Are you game Miss Leah?" I finally kiss her lips while pulling her atop me as close as I can get her. I can't seem to believe this beautiful woman is mine. Is she mine? I want her to be for sure. Not a doubt in my mind about that. There's only one way to make sure she understands how much I want her to be mine. Without words anyway.

\*\*\*\*\*\*\*\*\*\*\*\*\*\*\*\*\*\*\*

"Hey Karlie, how ya feeling today?"

"I'm great. So excited to get away from Aiden and go shopping!! And being with you is a definite bonus."

"Austin said that Aiden stayed with him the other night? What's up with that? Things okay?"

"Yes, I was being over emotional and he said the wrong thing once again. I blew up and kicked him out for the night. We're fine now; he's just hovering now and kissing up. Are you ready and excited?"

"Yes! Let's get a move on." I fake a smile knowing it would kill her to know how much I am actually dreading this whole trip. A bout of guilt washes over me for a second but I tamp it down and listen to Karlie chatter on about anything and everything.

At the first store we go to, Karlie squeals with delight as she sees the rows and rows of tiny person (as Austin called them) stuff. From baby carriers to clothes you could see forever it seems like. A whole lot of items I could really do without seeing. How did I get myself into this? Ugh.

"Leah isn't this just cutest little dress? Oh and there's matching shoes! I have to get these. What do you think? Purple or pink?" she says and shows me the most adorable frilly dress and sparkly little shoes. I can't help but see the loving smile on her face. I have to remember that this is Karlie's first time being pregnant and having the dreams of a child. She will be able to see her baby in a couple months and not go home to an empty nursery. Or feel empty.

What am I doing? I have to be more positive. I can't let my past pain and suffering hinder Karlie's experience, it isn't her fault. Ok so I need to breathe and clear all of the negative thoughts out of my mind. I have to put it all behind me even if just for the day to be here for Karlie the way she needs me to be. I breathe in and out. In and out.

Opening my eyes I see Karlie looking at me inquisitively. She has no idea the inner battle I was just having. If she only knew how my heart is breaking all over again looking at all the baby girl clothes and shoes I never got to buy. I wish I could tell her, would make this day quite a bit easier but she wouldn't have entrusted me in helping with her own child though. As hard as it is, I appreciate the trust more than I can explain. I have felt damaged since the accident and have just recently started to feel my heart and soul starting to mend. I know it has to do with Austin and everyone else in Colvin. I have to do this one day at a time. In this case, one store at a time.

"Are you okay Leah? You look like you're about to pass out."

"I'm good just deep in thought. Sorry, I like the purple."

"What theme are you doing the nursery in again?"

"Brown and pink polka dots with lots of sparkly things too."

"Perfect room for a princess? I didn't know you knew what you were having."

"Oops I wasn't supposed to say anything.  Aiden wanted to keep it a secret but it's been killing me not being able to tell anyone.  Don't tell Austin or he will tell Aiden and I will be in trouble."

Laughing I say with a big smile, "Your secret's safe with me.  But what's he going to say when you come home with all this girly stuff and he knows I was with you?"

"Crap, I hadn't thought about that.  Knowing him he already knows that I would let it slip."

"What about this little brown and white blanket?  It is so soft.  I think I'm going to get this for her.  Is that okay?  It still matches your theme."

"That's perfect because it's one that I came here to get.  I am so thankful you were willing to come with me today.  Do you think you will ever have a baby of your own?"

Trying not to show my panic I calmly smile and say, "I'm not sure.  We will just have to wait and see what God has in store for me."

"True. I wouldn't mind you giving me a niece or nephew. Or even both!"

"You're getting ahead of yourself Karlie. Austin is wonderful but a family with him? I don't know yet."

"I get it. I truly do. Aiden and I were in love since we were five but not everyone has that same love story."

"New subject. What else did you want to get today?"

"I need to order the crib, dresser, changing table, and closet organizer. If you want to go pay I will meet you in the car in a few once I get this order placed. Then we have to go eat because I am starving."

"Deal." I say and walk towards the checkout counter feeling surprisingly happy in the middle of this baby store. Maybe I can do this. But kids myself? I don't know that I can go that far. I can easily see Austin carrying around a baby boy or girl and being so happy. Just not sure I can see myself in the other parenting role in that same picture. I guess it's time to follow my own advice, only time will tell. I'll keep telling myself that. Only time will tell. Only time will tell.

## 30

"Hey Austin, Aiden have you heard from the girls today?" Mom asks from across the kitchen counter.

"No, I haven't heard from Leah. Have you heard from Karlie?"

"Not a word. I bet they're burning up my credit cards as we speak. They might need a trailer to bring all the stuff home. Great."

"Oh you love it and you know it. You have to admit you are as excited about this baby as Karlie is."

"I am, don't get me wrong, I just never realized how much crap you had to buy for such a little thing. It's less than two feet long and you have more gadgets and clothes and blankets than a normal person will use before it's graduating from college."

"Son, you had better get used to it. They only get more expensive the older they get!"

"Great. Good thing Karlie owns part of the breeding program; we might have to start cranking those babies out like never before!"

"Quit complaining Aiden, we all know you aren't hurting. You're just as bad as Karlie. Didn't you just buy a horse the other day for said "little thing"? And it's not even born yet."

"Shut it. I'm going back to my house. Thanks for lunch Mom. Austin, don't follow me this time." And he walks away cranky that I gave away his little secret purchase. He is excited and we all know it. We all know it because we're excited too. I can't wait to be an uncle. As I say that and picture myself holding a baby in my arms it isn't my niece or nephew, it's my own child. Leah and I's child. Whoa. That's far enough there dummy. Shaking my head I smile and walk away too. I need to get some work done and keep my mind off of babies and Leah. Way too soon.

*******************

"Hey handsome. Have a good day with Aiden?" I hear her voice coming in the living room as she opens my front door. I'm sitting on the couch trying to get a little research done on my laptop. As I hear her I look up and am stricken by how hot she looks.

I close my laptop and sit it on the coffee table. "Sure, did you have a good trip with Karlie?"

"Yes actually. Not sure why I was so stressed about it. It was great spending time with her."

"But you missed me, right?" I say wrapping my arms around her and pulling her close. I have really missed this girl.

"Without a doubt." She then leans her head up licking her lips inviting me to kiss them. She doesn't have to ask me twice. I press my lips to hers and pull her even closer. I hear her sigh and know she is just as affected by it as I am.

"I missed you so much." I whisper in her ear and nibble on the earlobe a bit. I know that drives her crazy because I can feel her shiver with need. Knowing this isn't going to end with a make-out session, I pick her up and carry her to my bedroom.

## 31

Things with Austin have been so great. We have been doing whatever we have been doing now for almost three months. We are half way through the six month period with the nursery ownership and neither of us has even thought about it. We have been enjoying being together and learning all we can about each other. And of course we have been falling in love. Life has gotten to a place where I can maybe see something more than this with him. I never realized things could be this good with another man. Even though Austin still doesn't know all about my accident, we have been able to talk a little more about things including marriage, kids, and a possible forever. While it still makes me squirm, I can carry on that conversation without having a panic attack. That is definite progress.

He left early this morning to go help his Dad with some chores on the 6AB leaving me in peace to get ready for another great day in our nursery. It amazes me how both of our outlooks on that ownership has changed since the first day. I couldn't have picked a better partner. Okay a better one away from the nursery too. That makes me smile and probably blush. Austin is amazing. Nothing could ruin this.

\*\*\*\*\*\*\*\*\*\*\*\*\*\*\*\*\*\*\*\*

"Hey Dad, I'm heading back to town. Leah's probably at the nursery by now and I need to get busy on the back sheds. They need shingles replaced before the next storm hits." I yell out as I walk out the door towards my pickup. I know Dad is shoeing a horse right now in the first horse stall so he could hear me.

"Okay. See you two tomorrow night for dinner. Tell Leah hello for us."

"I will do that and yes we will be there."

"Thanks for the help Son. Drive safe. Love you. Don't forget to stop off and tell your Mom goodbye."

"Bye Dad love you."

After stopping off at the big house, I'm on my way to the nursery in town. I am excited to see Leah. Any time away from her and I really do miss her. Things have been so great with us these past few months and I can't imagine life without her now. Being able to spend all day and night with her is amazing. Most couples couldn't handle being together so much, but I think that's what makes us work.

Pulling up to the nursery I can see Leah standing outside the front doors talking on the phone with someone and she doesn't look happy. She is pacing back and forth screaming actually. What could be so wrong that she'd be this upset? She hasn't gotten mad at the delivery guys before for making mistakes, what gives this time?

I get out of my pickup and walk to her. As I get to her I can hear better and realize she is talking to her dad. What in the world is going on here?

"Leah? What's wrong?" I ask trying to distract her. She looks at me and holds her hand up for me to stop. Ok, that's strange.

*******************

Hanging up my cell phone I am just numb. I can't believe this. And then of course Austin had to show up at the wrong time. I just can't believe this.

"Leah, what in the world is going on? Why were you so upset with your Dad? What is it Princess?" I ask trying to put my arms around her.

"That was my dad. I have to go back to New York." She says starting to look green. "Right now."

"What's going on?" I ask her as she pulls away from me. "What did your dad want that is so urgent that you have to go back there. Is he ill?"

"No." she says short. "He's fine."

"Then what Leah?" I'm starting to get a little scared. "Tell me."

"It's Lewis." She says in almost a whisper. With that she runs to her pickup and leaves before I can stop her.

I run to my pickup and follow to her house. I just don't understand what her ex has to do with her having to rush back to New York. Did she still love him? Please tell me she didn't still love the bastard who beat her up so badly.

Running to her door I find that she hasn't even shut it. I rush inside and up the stairs. I eventually find her sitting in the corner of the bathroom in a ball on the floor.

"Princess what is wrong? Why are you here like this?"

"Lewis was arrested and possibly killed his girlfriend." She says in a whisper afraid someone might hear her.

"What does that have to do with you Leah?" I ask trying to bring her into my arms again.

"I have to go testify." She says blankly. "About that night."

"Oh honey I am so sorry. I know you just want to move on from that night but it might help you to come to terms with it and move on." I say taking her face in my hands.

I touch my lips to her forehead and she stops crying. I have never felt so much emotion inside myself for one person in my life. She just looks so scared and it breaks my heart.

As she lifts her eyes and sees me looking at her so close, she says, "Will you go with me Austin?"

"You don't have to ask me that Leah. Of course I would go with you. I would go anywhere for you." I say as I finally get her pulled into my arms and sit on the side of the bathtub with her wrapped around me.

## 32

"Things will be fine while you're gone." Amelia says as we head to the pickup. "I'll watch over the nursery for you."

"Thanks Mom. We appreciate it. More than you know." I hear Austin say wondering if I should explain to her why we are rushing off to New York.

"Yes thank you Amelia." I say shakily. "We will call you when we land."

The two hour drive to Tulsa was long and silent. Neither one of us said much. We are both worried and scared of what things will be like when we get there.

As I look at Austin when he's getting our bags out of the pickup I wonder what I was thinking asking him to come along for this roller coaster. I still haven't told him about Shannon and I feel guiltier every time he kisses me. If he hears from someone else about her I will be devastated and he will be angry. He will think I couldn't trust him with that information. Even though I just can't talk about her. To anyone.

Dad meets us at the airport in New York and gives me a big hug and shakes Austin's hand.

"So good to see you again Austin. Thank you for helping Leah out."

"Anything she needs I will do it willingly." I hear Austin reply knowing he was saying it from the bottom of his heart. It warms my heart to hear so much devotion from one man.

"Well, let's get going. You have to be in the court room at nine in the morning Leah. You need some rest." Dad says as he opens my car door.

I just smile up at him and get in. Wondering how in the world I am going to face Lewis again after all this time. And talk about the tragic events of that night.

Not able to sleep I slip into the kitchen to find Dad sitting on a bar stool drinking a glass of milk.

"What are you doing up Dad? You need your rest too."

"I am just worried about you going in there tomorrow and having to reopen those old wounds. Have you told Austin the whole story Leah?" he asks knowing the answer.

"I told him almost all of it." I say then turn and get a glass out of the cabinet and fill it with water. "Not about her."

"Leah you have to tell him, he will hear it tomorrow. He will find out and it will hurt him that you didn't tell him first." He says moving to put his glass in the dishwasher. "Tell him Leah."

"I will dad when I'm ready. I still can't talk about her." I say trying to hold back the tears.

"If you want to be with this man Leah, you need to tell him everything. He deserves to know that you don't want to get married or have children." Dad says while backing out of the room.

"You don't want to get married or have children Leah?" I hear a familiar voice from behind my Dad. The very last voice I wanted to hear right now saying the very last words I ever wanted to hear.

"I'm sorry Flower. I'll leave you two and go to bed." Dad says and scurries off after kissing my forehead and squeezing Austin's shoulder.

Great, now I have no choice. Thanks Dad.

## 33

"Leah, what is your dad talking about. Is that really how you feel?" I ask as soon I know her dad is out of the room. I am in complete shock over what I just heard, hoping that I heard wrong.

"Austin that is something I am not so sure about. I was dead set against both when I first moved to Colvin." She says trying not to cry. "Now after meeting you, I don't know anymore."

"Well Leah, I need to know. I was considering proposing to you once we got back from here. I love you Leah and want to spend the rest of my life like we have been the past couple of months." I say hearing my voice crack a little and feeling myself start to tear up.

"Austin, I love you too! So much and that's why I have something I need to tell you that might help you understand more about me and why I am so confused about marriage and children." Leah says and motions us towards the living room sofa. "We need to sit down for this."

"Leah you're scaring me. Please just tell me." I say as I sit down next to her.

"Austin I haven't been able to talk about this since the day it happened. Dad knows because he was there but no one else. I didn't tell you the entire story of that night I was beaten so badly." She says trying to remain calm. "I was eight months pregnant but lost my little girl that night. Along with most of myself. Her name was Shannon and she would be five months old next week. I had her that night but she was already dead. I don't know if I will ever be able to go through being pregnant and not walking away without my child again."

I stand up and move to the window across the room. This is just too much to comprehend. She was a mother and that man took it away from her. How am I supposed to feel about all of this? How am I supposed to help her see that I want nothing but to love and protect her for the rest of her life? That I want a family to love and protect too?

"Austin, please say something." I hear her say through tears from the sofa. "You're scaring me. Please don't hate me for not telling you all of it before. I just couldn't talk about her. Until now."

I walk back to the couch and pull her up into my lap. I hear her start to sob and I myself let a few tears slip through my defenses.

"Leah, I love you and want nothing more from life than to marry you, have children with you, and protect you for the rest of my life." I say knowing full well that those things are what she fears the most. "But I will wait as long as I have to until you're ready. Even if you are never ready. As long as I have you then we will be happy for the rest of lives."

I look in her eyes as she lifts her head towards me and I see my future and my whole life in them. This is the woman I want to spend the rest of my life with. How do I get her to see that? How do I get her to want that too?

## 34

"How can that man still be walking the streets?" I hear Austin ask my father before I walk into the kitchen the next morning. It was a long emotionally draining night and it won't even hold a candle to what today will bring in the court room. Today is the day of the hearing. I don't know what to expect and I honestly don't know how I'm going to get through it. I haven't seen Lewis since the accident and I haven't wanted to either. I still don't.

"Leah was so upset that she didn't want to press charges as long as Lewis did as we asked and that was to quietly divorce her and give her a big settlement and ensured us that he would never come near her again or she would press charges." Her dad says feeling defeated. "And I was okay with that as long as that was what she wanted. There was no way she could have gone through a big trial having to recount it all."

"Still doesn't seem right. So, why are they calling her in today?" Austin asks not knowing I was behind him.

"Because the girlfriend kept in contact with me via email and had mentioned one time about that night. So, they dug deeper and found what they wanted. Now if I don't testify, he could go free. He will be up for life behind bars if he is convicted." I say putting my arms around him from behind.

"So he kills a woman and that isn't enough evidence to lock him up and throw away the key?" Austin asks jumping to his feet with his fists clenched.

"Austin, you have to settle down and understand that I am here for one reason and one reason only. Once this is over, I will never have a reason to come back here again. I will be free to move on. With you." I say looking into his eyes hoping to convey my feelings through them.

He wraps me in his arms and kisses the top of my head. Then walks off to shower leaving my father and me alone.

"You are doing the right thing baby, I promise."

"I know dad. I just wish it were easier."

"Flower, are you ready for this?" Dad asks after we're all ready to go.

"I don't have a choice Dad. They subpoenaed me. You know I wouldn't be here if it wasn't for that."

"Leah, I will be here through the whole thing. You know that right?" Austin says and wraps his arms around me from behind. He is trying to comfort me, I know, but his arms feel like chains.

I gently break away from his hold and walk to the cabinet and get out a glass and fill it. Taking large gulps, I swallow the water along with all the doubts I have about today.

Will Lewis be there? What will it be like to see him again? How will I feel or react? What will they ask me? Will they make me recount exactly what happened that night and after? Did he really kill her?

But most importantly, will Austin still love me and want to be with me after he hears the gory details? Will he finally see how broken I am? Panic is welling up inside of me so quickly that I feel like I am going to pass out.

"I'm okay. Let's get going. I will be better once this is over. We all will be. Are you sure you are ready for this you two?"

"Baby, we are fine. It's you we're worried about."

"Dad, I'll be fine. Seriously though, let's go."

On the drive to the courthouse I do nothing but stare out the window of Dad's car and honestly don't see a thing just a blur. My insides are all twisted up and my head is spinning. I never realized how far Dad lived away from everything until the trip was making me feel carsick. Except I know it's not car sickness.

Before I know it though, Dad has stopped the car in a parking spot across the street from the courthouse and I now have to face the reality of knowing there's nothing in the way of what I have to go do. Or where I have to go and be forced to retell that terrible night's story.

*******************

I don't know how Leah is keeping herself so calm. I am a nervous wreck just knowing what she is going to face in there. I'm not even the one having to do it. The whole drive over here she sat very still looking out the window. She never said a word. I didn't know what to say to her either, so I just kept quiet. Her father on the other hand, talked to whole way. I know he was trying to keep

Leah's mind off of the hearing but she didn't act like she heard a word he was saying.

She has got to be the strongest woman I've ever met, knowing what she's getting ready to face in there and is so calm and collected. I'm not sure how I'm going to handle hearing her relive those very painful moments or see her ex-husband for the first time since then.

I tuck Leah as close to my side as I can to show her and everyone around that she is untouchable. No one will hurt her while she is with me. Nearing the courthouse, we can see reporters everywhere. I have never seen so many people with cameras in one place. I feel Leah tense up as she sees them. It hits me that this is the reason she came to Colvin and has stayed. To get away from this craziness. Crazy ex. Crazy paparazzi.

Sensing that Leah is fighting to keep her composure and move forward, I tuck her closer still into my jacket and cover her head so that no one can be sure whom she is. I'm a nobody here in New York so maybe they won't realize it until she is safely inside. Safe inside? Who am I kidding? This whole thing is going to rock her to the core.

## 35

This whole circus is what I'm trying to avoid by being in Colvin. Oh good grief they are everywhere. I turn myself into Austin's side even more but it doesn't seem close enough. I hear him grumble to some of them who get too close but I don't think they know who I am thankfully.

Once we're inside the doors, it feels so quiet and calm. Outside is like a warzone. We just survived the warzone. But up those stairs in front of us and down a hall to the right is the courtroom where I will have to go through my own personal war. My own personal Hell.

"Are you okay Leah? That was a lot to handle." Dad says and lifts my face up to look at him. He is fighting back tears himself which makes me have to fight even harder to keep mine at bay. If I cry now I won't stop until next week and might flood the courthouse.

"I'm okay dad. Really. Let's go." He nods at me and motions for me to go up the stairs. Once we get to the courtroom doors he opens them and looks in first to see whom is inside before allowing me to go in. Lewis must not be in there yet. Yet.

I walk inside the doors and see a row of seats on each side of me leading up towards the judge's bench. Not even the judge is in here right now. We must be early. Most likely what Dad had planned on. Getting me in before I have to make a grand entrance with everyone else is inside. Thank you Dad. I have to remember to thank him after this nightmare is over.

Dad sits in one of the back seats and motions for me to follow and sit next to him. Austin sits on the other side of me. Flanked by the most wonderful men I have ever met. I feel calmer and protected knowing they are here. Amidst this craziness we are in the middle of, I do feel calm. Surprisingly calm. I am sitting here wondering why exactly that is when Austin takes my hand and squeezes it tight and Dad puts his arm around my shoulders from his side. That explains the calmness. I know that once this is all over I will still have so much happiness to go home to. I just need to get through Lewis' arrival.

I spoke too soon. On the far right side of the judge's bench, doors open and in comes a man dressed in a policeman's uniform. And then one dressed in stripes. My stomach drops as I see his face looking around the room as if he is searching for someone. Then his eyes stop on me and he looks so sad and lowers his head to the ground.

He can't look at me? That is far from what I expected. The last time I saw this man, he was belligerent and violent, but this one across the room now is the polar opposite. He is almost acting like he's broken.

"The prosecution calls Leah Stampley Frankle to the stand."

I look up out of my stupor not sure how long I was in it as I hear my name. It sounds so foreign being said by the district attorney. His voice is loud and deep cutting through the silence surrounding the room. Austin squeezes my hand a little tighter and stands up to allow my exit from the row of seats. Dad whispers his love to me from the other side which makes me feel even better than I did before. I actually feel as if I can get through this. I walk forward feeling everyone's eyes on me as I draw nearer to the witness stand.

Reaching the step I turn into the policeman trying to help me in and smile as much of a smile as I can muster. I take my seat and prepare for the worst and pray this is over soon.

"Mrs. Frankle, can I call you Leah?" District Attorney Greg Bort asks. I nod my head and whisper out a yes. "Could you recount to us what happened the night of June 4, 2013?"

I start telling my story of that horrible night without looking at Lewis. I try my hardest not to let much emotion slip out in any other form than words. But when the D.A. asks me about Shannon I can't help but let the tears and emotion surface.

"She died that night from too much trauma. My baby girl died." I sob and cover my face with my hands and lower my head. Unable to control myself any longer, the D.A. sees that I can no longer go on and dismisses me. They all know that's the end of my story. At least my story with Lewis.

The policeman helps me off the stand again but I don't look up this time because I don't want anyone to see me so upset. Especially not Lewis. I want him to think I am doing just fine without him. Which I am. I want him to pay for what he did. And this time I believe he will.

When I get back to my seat, Austin is there with open arms. I collapse into them and feel him kiss the top of my head. I silently say a big "thank you" to Mom and Grandpa for pushing Austin and I together. I know they are the ones behind it. Nothing else could explain finding him when my life was shattered and having him here to mend me.

"I don't want to hear any more of this Austin. Will you take me outside? Dad, you can stay in here but I can't." I hug Dad and kiss his cheek. I know it's best for me to leave the room now. I have to put an end to this tragedy and pain. Time to move on and let all the pain go.

"Leah I am so proud of you. You were so strong up there. That had to be so hard on you." Austin says after we are safely outside the courtroom. He wraps me in his arms and squeezes me tightly. Where has this man been my whole life? He makes my insides so happy. My heart is full even after having to recount the pain of losing my little girl.

"Thank you. It was tough and I am so thankful it's over."

"Let's go get some coffee from down the hall while we wait for your Dad. You wouldn't think there's much else to say. We were in there for an hour and a half. Everyone delivered their sides and presented the evidence."

"Did you see the pictures of me from that night?"

"No, from where I was sitting they weren't visible. Do you want me to see them?"

"No. Absolutely not. I was worried the whole time that you were going to see them and change how you look at me. I was so broken."

"Nothing could make me think anything but what I already do about you. And I think you are amazing and I love you Leah."

"Austin, please don't say those words just to make me feel better. Wait until you really mean them."

"I do mean them Leah. More than I can explain." And he lifts my chin to kiss me. His lips are soft and I hear myself sigh. If this were a movie I would do the leg pop thing. I smile and know this is my future. And will finally be amazing without the fears I have had leading up to it.

## 36

"He got life. He won't be able to hurt anyone ever again. It's over Leah, all over. Now you can move on with your life. Forget about him and live a much better life with Austin." Dad says as he comes to us after exiting the courtroom. He has a pleased look on his face so things must have gone the way they should.

"Thank you two for coming with me today. I couldn't have done any of that without you."

"Flower, I would do anything for you. I believe Austin would too. Now just promise me you will go back to Colvin and forget about New York. Forget about all the hurt and pain you have been through. Start over. Maybe even get married again and have more babies?"

"In due time Dad. Let me breathe that Oklahoma air and feel the sun on my skin without having to look over my shoulder for Lewis or the past I had. I just can't get over how different he looked in there. He looks completely broken. I think he actually realizes what he did. To both of us women. And the baby."

"He should look broken Leah. He just about broke you. Only you would still find compassion for a monster like that. That's one of main reasons I love you so much. Your heart is so big."

"Can we go home now and forget about all of this?"

"We can do whatever you want Flower. How about we get some lunch at your favorite restaurant?"

"The Grill, that sounds fabulous Dad! Austin, you are going to love it."

"I have eaten at one in Las Vegas and it was amazing."

"This one's even better." We start towards the front stair case before we hear someone from behind us say my name. Now what? I thought this was over. I turn to see a gentleman in an expensive looking suit walking towards me. I can't tell if he is irritated or just unsure of my identity.

"Mrs. Frankle, could I have a moment of your time?" We all turn around and face the unknown gentleman. "Mr. Frankle would like a moment with you before he is taken to the prison. If you are up for it that is. No one can force you and you have every right to refuse his request."

I look at Dad then Austin trying to see what they are thinking of this request.

"Flower you don't owe him anything. You don't have to do this."

"Leah please be sure. This is something you can't undo. If you're sure, go. We will be here waiting for you when you're done. We love you." Austin kisses my forehead and urges me to follow the suited man.

I realize it's the only way I will forever be over this whole ordeal. "Yes, I will see him. But only for a few minutes." I follow Lewis' attorney down the hall and into a small room with policemen standing around a man that I know I don't want to see. A man that doesn't even look like the man I was married to. Time has not been good to the man I vowed to love and cherish 'til death do us part.

"Leah, thank you for coming. I know it's more than I should ever ask of you but I need to get a few things out in the open before I'm taken to prison. I'm going to just say it and get it out. Please just listen. Leah, I am so sorry about what I did to you. You were the best thing that ever happened to me and I blew it big time. I let alcohol and depression get the best of me. By doing that I demolished the best part of me. You and our little girl. I know you deserve so much more out of life than what we had and of course you deserve to be a mother more than anything. I took that away from you in a drunken rage and I will forever be saddened to know I took the one thing that would have made you happy away. Please know that I did love you and you are an amazing person and deserve the world. Please be happy Leah." Lewis says tearing up between words. "Ok guys I'm done."

And just like that Lewis is hauled away in cuffs while I stay in this small room trying to absorb all of what he said. I can finally breathe after all of these months. I feel tears starting to well up behind my eyes but I take a deep breath, one that I haven't been able to take for a very long time and know it is finally over. Know I am safe. Know I am ready for what's ahead.

## 37

"Before we go back to Colvin, I need to go somewhere. But I can go alone."

"Leah, you don't have to go there alone. I'll come with you if you want me to. Just ask." Austin says and pulls me into his arms. He must have seen the pain on my face as I was envisioning going to Shannon and Mom's graves.

"Would you really go with me Austin? I want them to both meet you. I know that sounds crazy but I feel like they are there at the cemetery."

"It's not crazy at all Leah. Of course I'll go with you. They are a part of you. A big part that I want to meet too."

As we drive down that familiar tree and headstone lined road that still makes my insides do jumping jacks, I can't help but remember how it felt that day. The day that I had to bury and say goodbye to the two most important females in my life, especially my little girl. I know she will always be in my heat but I still feel the pain when I come here. It has been a bit easier not living in the same town as her headstone, but on the other hand I feel guilty too because I left her behind.

"Penny for your thoughts."

"I was just remembering how it felt that day when I buried Shannon. And how guilty I sometimes feel for leaving her behind and moving to Colvin."

"Leah, you can't feel that way. She isn't here anyway. It's just a piece of stone. She's in Heaven with your Mom. You shouldn't feel guilty."

"I know all of this, I really do. It's just hard knowing I can't go see her whenever I want anymore. I used to come here almost every day."

"Leah, I'm so sorry." Austin says as we pull up to the row where I know I will find my little angel. We stop to the right of the large sycamore tree and the left of the stone fountain. Directly ahead about 24 ½ paces you will find her small headstone sitting next to my parents' large one.

When we approach the spot I see there are fresh flowers on both graves. Gerber daisies on Mom's and little pink roses on Shannon's. Dad. He must still come here pretty often. They don't look wilted at all. I touch the ones on Mom's grave and instantly feel her presence. A wave of relief washes over me and I can't help but look up at Austin to see if he's feeling this too. It feels as if someone is putting their arms around me which helps me to relax. Even the tightness around my heart eases a little. I realize that Mom is here to comfort me the only way that she can now. She's here to let me know that it's all okay. That I'm okay now. When she was alive she always knew just what to say and the exact moment to say it. It was like she had a super power when it came to an upset person. That was the type of mother I had hoped to be. Maybe still do hope to be. Could I really be changing my mind about having more children? With Austin?

"Mom, this is Austin. I'm sure you were behind our meeting along with Grandpa. For that I want to say thank you. I don't think we would have found each other any other way. I love him and I'm sure you would have too. Grandpa sure did." I smile and look up at

Austin and roll my eyes. He smiles back with that adorable and heartwarming smile I love so much.

"Ma'am, I can't begin to tell you how happy I am that I found your daughter. I promise that I will take very good care of her." He smiles again and looks down at me while squeezing my shoulder.

"That was so sweet Austin. Thank you." I take a few steps to the left to Shannon's grave. As I do tears start to form in my eyes but I also still feel that calming sensation that I felt before. Austin senses my hesitation and puts his arm around my waist and pulls me closer to his side. I just smile up at him and take a deep breath.

"Shannon, baby girl, this is Austin. You would have really liked him. He makes Mommy very happy and Mommy loves him very much. I love you and miss you more than words can say." I break down sobbing this time and feel Austin pulling me all the way into his arms allowing me to fall apart.

"Shannon, your Mama loves you and I also promise you that I will take very good care of her."

I step out of his arms and turn to look at his handsome face. "Can I have a moment alone?" He nods and walks back to the car. I could tell he was hesitant to leave me alone, but knew it was best if he did.

"Well baby, what do you think? He's a wonderful man. Do you think Mommy should keep him? I love him so much Shannon. He's very kind, sweet, loving and I think he loves me too. I wish you could be here to meet him. He would have loved you too. What do you think about Mommy giving you a little brother or little sister? What about Austin being your Daddy? I really wish you were here to give me the answers I need. I'm so confused about this stuff." As I say that last part and start to fall apart again, I get an even stronger calming sensation as if someone small was putting their arms around my neck. I feel deep inside my heart that it's Shannon giving me the answers I need. She seems happy with Austin and us being together. I will take this as a yes or at least I want to believe it's her telling me yes.

With my heart feeling better than it has in a long time, I kiss my fingers and place them on Shannon's headstone exactly where her name is engraved. I stand up, take a deep breath and walk back to the car. Towards Austin and our future together.

\*\*\*\*\*\*\*\*\*\*\*\*\*\*\*\*\*\*\*

Leaving Leah up there at the graves alone was torture. I wanted nothing more than to stand there holding her all day while she was so upset. I know it's tough on her being at Shannon's grave but also know that she needs to be alone up there to sort out her feelings for me and our future. Maybe then she won't feel so guilty about moving on. I should get a memorial site set up for her back home in Colvin so that she can go visit Shannon anytime she wants to again. Where should I put it? I'll have to talk to Mom about it when we get back. Well, after Leah explains her past to everyone. I wouldn't want to let the cat out of the bag before she has a chance to. She wouldn't be happy about that.

## 38

"Are you sure you are ready to do this Leah? There's no rush."

"Austin, I have to do this. I have to get all of this out in the open so I can finally move on. Move on completely."

"Okay, well just call me when they leave. I'll be at the 6AB. I love you. They love. Nothing to be nervous about."

"Who said I was nervous?" I say smiling and trying to breathe normally. If my hands weren't shaking I might be able to pull it off.

"Leah, it will all be fine. I love you." And he kisses me and leaves but as he does I see Amelia's SUV pull into the spot where his pickup used to be. Well here goes. Ready or not.

"Thank you all for coming tonight. There's a lot we need to catch up on. And while we still can before that baby comes. " I say to all the important women in my life but looking directly at Karlie's swollen mid-section. As I look around at Amelia, Audrey and Karlie I realize that I am very blessed to have them. They have enveloped me into their family without really knowing much about me. I wonder if they will still feel that way later tonight after I finally tell everyone about the accident, Shannon and the trial in New York.

Lord please be with me while I do this. I am going to need your help to make it through.

"Ladies, grab a plate, food, and a glass of wine." Motioning towards the kitchen island, I too grab a glass of wine. I gulp it all down in a rush knowing I need a little bit of extra courage to get through this. Amelia must see the uneasiness written all over my face because she squeezes my shoulder as she walks by.

Once all the ladies are seated and occupied, I begin my rehearsed speech. Austin helped me come up with the best way to present it and deliver such a terrible story. I just pray we came up with the best approach. Well here goes.

"I wanted you all to come tonight because Austin and I are wanting to move forward with our relationship and I don't feel that I deserve that until I have been completely honest with all of you about what happened in my life before I came to Colvin a few months ago."

"Leah, we don't need to know anything, we love you for who you are. We know you are a wonderful person and are so very good to my son."

"Amelia, I appreciate that but you all need to know a few pieces of information about me and you might understand a little more about why I am the way that I am. Or had been. Before I came to Colvin, as you all know, I was married to Lewis Frankle. He and I lived in a big high-rise on the Upper East Side in New York. He was a pitcher for the Yankees. He also had an injury that kept him from playing the previous and current seasons. He became very depressed and angry turning to alcohol as a solution. He would come home after a loss and be very intoxicated. He never got violent with me until one night. I tried to help him up the stairs and to bed but he tossed me down the stairs which I fell clear to the bottom of. I was also eight months pregnant." I could tell by the gasps and looks on their faces that things were starting to make sense to them.

"Oh Leah, I'm so sorry something like that happened to you."

"I'm not finished. My baby girl didn't make it. She died that night. Shannon died that night. My father talked to Lewis and made a quiet deal with him that ensured he would stay away from me forever and keep our problems and the accident out of the media. I moved into my Dad's and Lewis sold our house. We divorced quickly and a few days after my casts came off I got the call from Roger Yasser. The rest of the story you all know."

"That's when you met Austin."

"Yes. When I first met him I didn't want anything to do with a man or ever to get married and have kids again. I was too raw but Austin and all of Colvin has helped me to heal on the inside too."

"What did you have to run to New York for so quickly last week?"

"Lewis was arrested and charged with killing his girlfriend and since I had been married to him I was called to testify to his character. It was then that my Dad had to tell the authorities about that horrible night. Once they figured that out they also tacked attempted murder and a bunch more onto his sentence because of my testimony. It was the hardest thing I think I have ever had to do, besides losing Shannon. Afterwards, he asked to see me and actually apologized for what he had done. It helped to close the doors from that awful night. I am now ready and able to move on with Austin."

"What about getting married again and having more children?" I knew Amelia would be the one to ask that. I look her way and smile knowing my answer is coming straight from my mended heart.

"I would like nothing more. I love Austin more than I ever thought I could love one person."

"I believe the feelings are mutual. We might all be sisters! Audrey, what do you think about having two sister in laws?"

"I think its great Karlie. But we do still have Aaron to marry off too!"

"Can we lighten the atmosphere and have a good time now?" I ask praying they agree. Enough of the gloom and doom. On with the happily ever after stuff.

Looking around this room again I feel as if I am finally home and have a family to call my own. Missing Mama a little more than usual, I put my hand over my heart and whisper to her that I love her.

"She would be so proud of the woman you have become Leah. Just as I am of the woman that holds my middle son's heart. Welcome to our family." Amelia says and gives me a big hug. My heart is just so full of love and happiness right now I'm not sure how I will go on. I smile and wipe tears away and hug her back.

## 39

"Hey Dad. How's it going?"

"Austin. It's going pretty good. Just watching a little TV before your Mama gets back and makes me turn it off. She doesn't take to kind to these old westerns I like." He says smiling as he visualizes Mom's disdain for his old movies. She never has liked them, even when I was a child she wouldn't let us watch them with him. Says there's too much violence. Wonder how she feels about movies today. I bet she bans all movies in this house now. That makes me smile too.

"She never has liked them."

"So what did they all meet at Leah's for tonight? Do you know?"

"Yes actually I do. Leah wanted to talk to all the ladies in the family and explain her past to them. She feels that she's ready to open up to them and that maybe it would help them to understand him a little bit more too."

"What would she need understood about? We all know she was married before, that's no big deal to us."

"It's a lot more than that Dad. Leah was eight months pregnant and her husband came home drunk and violent. He shoved her down the stairs leaving her battered and bruised. She also lost the baby that night."

"Oh my goodness. That is so terrible. Oh my, no wonder she has been so spooked."

"That's the main reason she wanted to explain it to the important people in her life, so they understood why she was so hesitant about me and our future."

"Wow, I can definitely understand. That poor girl. I hope you understand how much she needs you Son."

"I do and I will never ever let her hurt like that again."

"You're a good man Austin. I believe she was meant to come find you here."

"Same here. Let's watch some shoot 'em up bang bang before Mom gets home!" I smile over at Dad and receive the same smile back.

*******************

"So how did it go with the girls? Do you feel better now?"

"It was great actually. I do feel better. I'm glad I did it. Did you tell the guys?"

"No. The girls will tell them. I just told Dad. We're supposed to go to dinner later this week with them at Mom's or Karlie's."

"Okay, let me know when. Dad called earlier before the girls came and he says that Lewis was transferred to prison in Attica. That's where he will serve out his sentence."

"That's great to hear. Now we can move on. Right?" I say and pull her into my arms.

"Right. I love you Austin." After she says those three little words that can clear any gray skies, I kiss her lips and attempt to convey to this woman just how much I love her.

"Are you trying to distract me Mr.?"

"Why yes I am Princess. Are you down for that?"

She kisses my cheek and then runs her hands down my chest stopping just above my waist band. I look down at her and see the love in her eyes. Nothing could beat a moment like this. Seeing the love and feeling the love of a wonderful woman.

## 40

"Are we ever going to do anything that doesn't involve a bed Austin?" I say teasing him the next morning. "Not that I am complaining but we really should have a life outside the bedroom."

"What would you like to do then? We could go fishing or camping. Or horseback riding."

"I don't know how to ride a horse, you know that."

"Doesn't mean you can't learn ya know. I taught Aiden and Audrey how to ride, I'm sure I could handle you."

"You could handle me all right, that's not what I was thinking about."

"Funny. And you wonder why we don't leave the bedroom but to go to work."

"No, seriously. You think you could teach me to ride?"

"Sure. Is that what you want to do on this fine Saturday?"

"Yes. I think."

"You think? What are you scared of?"

"Falling off. Getting trampled. You know, the normal stuff."

"Honey, you will not fall off of Spook or get trampled by him. He moves at the speed of a tortoise and I think you could walk underneath him and not get trampled."

"Spook? Why does he have that kind of a name then?" I say a little scared to know the answer and wrap myself up in the sheet. I'm unsure if I want to spend a day on top of a horse named Spook.

"Aiden and Karlie named him when they were like fifteen or something. I don't remember when we got that horse. Karlie thought it would be funny to name him something like that. You know like Smalls for a big horse or Big Guy for a small one?"

"Ah gotcha. Ok, so what do I wear?"

"What you're wearing now is good for me." Austin says and pulls the sheet away from me leaving me standing in the middle of the room with not even a stitch of clothing on.

"You are such a funny guy. Definitely a guy. What CLOTHES should I wear?"

"Ok ok ok. If you have to put some clothes on just wear jeans and a t-shirt. I'm sure Audrey or Mom has a pair of boots you could borrow. We need to get you some of your own though. You will get addicted to riding after spending a day with me on horseback." He stands up naked also and smiles as he walks away towards the shower.

That man is going to be the death of me. Or just what I have been waiting for. Definitely what I have been dreaming about my whole life. I smile and walk to join him in the shower. Ok, at least it's not the bed.

*******************

"You are going to teach her to ride on Spook? You could always use a horse that isn't asleep at the wheel. You do know he is like a hundred years old."

"Yes, that's the point. Start her on one that's not going to quote unquote spook her."

"You are pretty clever sometimes big brother."

"You are just figuring this out? Anyways, does Karlie have some boots Leah can borrow today? I need to get her some but we didn't want to go shopping today. Maybe I'll take her to Tulsa next week shopping. We can close the nursery and make an overnight trip out of it."

"Wow, who are you and what have you done with my workaholic big brother?"

"Ha ha. Now how about those boots smart ass?"

## 41

"So, how does that feel?" Austin asks after he helped me get situated on top of Spook.

"It feels good. I think." Smiling back at him I know he wants this day to go perfectly. I won't tell him that I am scared to death or that this saddle is hard. I would rather be in bed. Or the shower. Whose idea was it that we should do something other than have sex?

"Over that hill just past the corral you'll be able to see for hundreds of miles."

"Ok, lead the way." I say trying to sound okay with this. Although I am thinking I must have lost my mind for a second when I agreed to this.

"Alright, just kick his sides lightly and he will go. Like this, watch me."

"Ok here goes." I kick my heels into the horse's sides expecting to get bucked off. I know my eyes are closed as I wait to hit the ground.

"Leah? Why are your eyes closed? You can't see the sights with them closed all day." I open my eyes to see him smiling at me. Ok, maybe he does know what he's doing. I look down at the horse and see that we have actually moved forward and are slowly and very gently moving. Wow. I can't even tell I'm moving. Maybe this will be fun after all.

I look up at Austin and know that he sees how amazed I am at this whole horseback riding thing. He knew all along it was going to be great; I just had to be a brat like always I guess.

About ten minutes later we reach the top of the hill he was talking about and it is the most breathtaking scene I have ever seen. It looks like it's out of an artist's masterpiece. It's amazing. Green grass meets the most gorgeous blue sky with touches of white clouds. Wow. Just spectacular.

"You guys own all of this?"

"Yes, our property line is just past where you can see. What do you think?"

"I think its spectacular Austin. Your family has the most breathtaking views."

"It's pretty awesome. Aiden and I used to come up here a lot when we were upset about something growing up. It's a good place to clear your head."

"I can only imagine. It's just so amazing. Like something artists dream of painting."

"Actually, we have been thinking about hiring someone to come and do a painting from this spot. Aiden and Karlie have a lot of pictures in their house from this spot and various spots around the ranch. I'm sure you've seen them."

"I can only imagine how many hundreds of pictures she has taken up here. She could probably spend hours here."

"We like to joke with them that the baby was probably conceived up here."

"I wouldn't doubt it. It's gorgeous."

"Yes it is." I look back at Austin to find him not looking at the view but at me. Could this man get any better?

"The view Austin."

"That too. I love you Leah. Have I told you that today?"

"Yes, several times. And I love you too. Thank you for bringing me here." As I say that my stomach lets out a loud growl making Austin smile and laugh.

"Hungry my dear? Would you like to see what Mom has sent for our lunch?"

"Oh yes!" I help Austin unload the basket and blanket off of his horse. I spread the blanket out still amazed by the view from up here.

"Egg salad sandwiches, pasta salad, freshly made wheat bread, veggies straight from the garden, and looks like lemonade. Sound good?"

"Sounds better than good. Your Mom is awesome!"

"She kinda feels the same about you Leah. I have never seen her take to someone new quite like she has you."

"Not even Karlie?"

"Karlie wasn't new. We have known her since she was five."

"Oh ya. It's still so strange to know that Karlie and I knew each other and worked together in big cities all over the world and now we're both in Colvin, Oklahoma deeply in love with two rowdy cowboy brothers."

"Rowdy? Maybe Aiden but not me." He says with a mischievous grin on his face.

"Oh you are rowdy too my dear. Maybe more than Aiden. I have heard some of the stories."

"Nah, that was probably Aaron."

"Speaking of Aaron, why isn't he ever here?"

"He lives in Denver."

"Doesn't come home much?"

"He doesn't feel the same way about Colvin as Aiden and I do. He likes the hustle and bustle of the big city. Must have been the same for you and Karlie for all those years you were there."

"Yes, it can get under your skin. But if you have something like this to come back to, why would you want to stay away?"

"He never had much to do with the ranch. He always wanted to be in the garage building things. He built all of the chicken coops and bird houses mom could ever want. I was doing the landscaping around the places he was building while Aiden was off getting the animals to fill them."

"That's funny. You three are so different but you figured out how to make it work together. I always wanted a sibling when I was growing up but once Mama died I knew Dad wouldn't want to remarry again. He was too devastated."

"Has he ever dated?"

"Not that I know of. He worked too much. Maybe now that he's retired he will. Who knows. Know any single older women?"

"Um, not really. Never really looked at women like that until I met my little flower. Isn't that what your Dad calls you?"

"Yes and I hate it. He has called me that since I was little because I always loved flowers."

"Maybe he knew you would end up here too. You know I kinda owe your Grandpa. A lot. If he hadn't have divided up the nursery ownership, I probably wouldn't have ever met you again."

"Probably not. I had almost forgotten about coming here when I was younger."

"Forgotten? How could you have forgotten about a hunk like me? You know I always did have a monster sized crush on you. I was always so excited when summer break would come around because you would be here to stay for a few months."

"Why didn't you ever tell me that?"

"I was too shy. And you were a big city girl and I never thought I had a chance with you. I was a dumb hick, your words exactly. I wasn't going to make a fool of myself like that."

"I'm sorry I called you a dumb hick. I was just being mean. I had a gigantic crush on you too but I didn't think you could stand me. How funny. We had chemistry back then too. No wonder everyone knew we would be a perfect match."

"This dumb hick is so happy to have his big city girl back in his life. Even if she did take away half of his nursery. You know I wanted to buy it from Jack didn't you?"

"No, I thought he was just being nice since you had worked for him all those years."

"That too I would imagine, but I did want to purchase it. Not sure he ever knew that though. I had been working on the business plan and all that stuff with Aaron the past couple of years actually. I was just never sure it was good enough to get Jack's approval so I never thought it was done."

"I guess he knew you better than you did. He knew you were the best part of Stampley's. That is until he brought me in. Now of course I am." I laugh a hearty laugh that feels so good to get out. Now that the laughter comes so easily it amazes me. How have I gone so long without it?

"That's true." He smiles and kisses my lips. "I love hearing you laugh."

"Well, I am starting to miss being up on that horse. Are you ready to head back?"

"You lead, I'll follow. My turn to enjoy the view."

"This could be fun." I say and mount my horse just as Austin had showed me. So much easier this time. I could really get used to this.

"I knew you would like it." He smiles and away we go back towards the corrals.

## 42

"So, how do you feel? Sore?" Karlie asks once I dismount at the barn. She stands there more pregnant than I have ever seen someone to be but she still looks so beautiful. She always has been beautiful.

"Great. A little sore yes, but not bad. How are you feeling is the more important question. Aren't you due anytime now?"

"Yes. Next week actually. I feel like a house and like I've been preggo for a year!"

"It will all be worth it soon. Just hang in there."

"It doesn't make you uncomfortable talking about it with me?"

"No. Actually it kinda makes me feel better. Something positive. Since the trial I have been able to put it all behind me and move on."

"That's awesome Leah. I am so happy to have you here with us. Especially with how happy you have made Austin."

"He has made me just as happy. He has actually made me whole again." I smile and look over towards where the guys are unsaddling the horses and feeding them in the barn.

"Do you think you two will get married and have babies soon?"

"I really don't know. We are enjoying each other and this new thing we have right now. No rush ya know?"

"I do. And I totally understand it. Well, I have to go sit back down in the recliner. My ankles have been swelling a lot and the doctor says I have to keep my feet elevated as much as possible. I just wanted to see how your first ride went. Once I'm not preggo anymore we have to go for a ride together."

"Deal. Talk to you later. Take care of yourself Karlie."

"Bye! Austin, take care of her for me."

"I will Karlie, bye."

"I think she's going to make a great mother."

"Yes, she is. Is that something you want to try again Leah? Someday?"

"The more I think about it the more I think it might be a good thing. But I'm just not ready yet."

"I understand and I'm not pushing, I was just curious."

"Don't give up on me yet." I smile and wrap my arms around him and breathe in his scent. This man's scent is something I don't think I could ever get tired of inhaling.

"Never baby never."

## 43

The next day we are all out at the 6AB again but this time we are setting up for Karlie and Aiden's surprise baby shower. They have no idea it's coming and no idea that all of us are here.

"They are on their way up. They think we are here to have dinner together." Austin says as he hangs up the phone. He must have just called Aiden and told them to get up here.

"Karlie is going to cry. You all know that right?" I ask knowing she is so emotional right now that this will send her overboard.

"We have lots of tissues handy." Laughs Amelia as she grabs a box and sets them in front of her.

"Karlie's going to love it though." Audrey says from beside Amelia. Amelia puts her arm around Audrey's waist and smiles back. It is obvious how much Amelia loves her children. It's moments like this that make me miss my own mother. She would have loved Amelia. And Austin.

"They're here. Everyone into the living room and quiet." AJ yells and ushers everyone into the room and away from the front door.

"Mom? Dad? Austin? Where is everyone?" We hear Aiden say as they walk inside the house.

"Leah? Amelia? Audrey? Aiden I thought they said we were supposed to be here for dinner?"

"That's what Austin said on the phone just now."

"SURPRISE!!" We all yell as they walk into the living room where we're all hiding in the dark.

"Oh my goodness! What have you all done?" Karlie says while wrapped around Aiden sobbing into his chest. He has the biggest smile on his face and rubs her back.

"Are you okay Karlie?" Amelia asks and hands her a box of tissues. "We thought you would be happy to have a baby shower. Were we wrong?"

"No, it's so nice of you all. I just can't believe you all did this. Mom? How did you keep this from me too?" Karlie says and hugs her mom.

"We all knew this was something you wanted but wouldn't ask for. So, here we all are." Ella Mae says sweetly while rubbing Karlie's back. I see where Karlie gets her sweet and caring nature.

"Thank you all so much. This means the world to both of us." Karlie finally says once she stops crying. "No more tears now."

"Okay well, let's get to the presents then." Says Aiden like a little child at Christmastime.

"Aiden! Don't be rude." Karlie yells over at him.

"It's okay Karlie; we can do the presents whenever you want. This is your party." Amelia says as she walks to the dining room where the gifts had been taken.

"My kind of party!" Aiden says laughing as he sits in one of the two chairs in front of the pile of gifts.

"Looks like I'm going to have two children next week!" Karlie laughs and sits next to him shaking her head.

"He's one that will never grow up though." Ella Mae says and laughs along with them. She hands Karlie the first gift.

"Open this one first. It's from me." Karlie looks up at her mom once she hands the gift to her and smiles trying not to cry again.

"Okay, what do we have in here?" She pulls the wrapping paper apart slowly while Aiden tries to rip it off. They look like two children fighting over a Christmas gift. Everyone chuckles to see them.

Karlie opens up a box that contains a baby blanket made out of her father's favorite shirts. The very same shirts Karlie used to love to wear to bed as she was growing up.

"Mom this is so…" And she's crying again. This might be the longest gift unwrapping ever seen. If she cries after everyone we might still be here next week when the baby is born.

"You always loved those shirts so much growing up so I thought maybe your little girl or boy would love them too." Ella Mae says and hugs both expectant parents.

"Well, we have a bit of a surprise for you too." Karlie says and stands up beside Aiden. All eyes are on them again.

"We have known the gender of the baby for a couple of months now but were waiting for the right time to tell you. When a good time never really came up, we just thought it would be best to wait until the birth." Aiden says and slips his arm around Karlie.

"Out with it already. There are a ton of gifts and a ton of food waiting in that kitchen!" AJ yells and laughs from the far corner. He winks at Karlie and Aiden once they look his way smiling.

"We are having a little Princess." Karlie says with so much excitement. She has a big smile on her face and she might actually be crying again.

"A granddaughter!! AJ and Ella Mae did you hear that?? We are going to have a granddaughter!"

"Oh honey! We are so proud of you." Ella Mae says and wraps her arms around Karlie and Aiden at the same time. The embrace looked awkward but we all knew she just loved them too much to hug separately.

"Ok, now that the cat's out of the bag, can we get back on track here?" Aiden says and winks at his dad still standing over in the far corner. A big guy like him isn't really into lovey dovey stuff but also wouldn't miss this for the world.

I look over at Austin and see how happy he looks standing here watching his little brother and sister in law open gifts for his soon to be niece. I just wonder if I will ever be able to give him his own child. He would make such a wonderful father and that would be one loved child with a loving family like he has here in this room.

Austin looks down at me and squeezes my waist and kisses my forehead. I can definitely get used to the sparks this man sends through me with something as simple as a kiss on the forehead.

"I love you." He whispers into my ear and smiles. Looking back at the gift opening we see that they are to the gift that we gave them. I bought the blanket in Tulsa and Austin picked out the bedding from the same store afterwards. We also got the baby a baby book that has flowers on it that depict the exact ones that grow by the creek where Karlie and Aiden love to go. Karlie cries once again when she sees the book.

"We know your Dad can't be here but wanted to make sure he was a big part of the baby's life too." Austin says while squeezing my waist again.

"It's perfect you two." Karlie is crying so hard now it's tough to even understand her words.

"Okay, I think it's time for the food now before Karlie dehydrates herself from all these tears." We all hear AJ say from his special corner spot. Everyone chuckles and heads to the kitchen.

"The outside patio is set for dinner. Go on out while the ladies and I bring the food out." Amelia says while walking into the kitchen. Not wanting everyone in the actual kitchen she stands in the doorway directing traffic.

"Leah, the book was a perfect choice. With you two being flower people and of course with the flowers being by the creek. We love it so much!" Karlie says and hugs me. It feels so wonderful to be a part of this family's day.

"You are very welcome. Austin and I both thought it was a great match." I say and hug her back.

"Have I told you lately how happy I am to have you back in my life?"

"Karlie, you tell me all the time. Don't worry. I feel the same way and I'm not going anywhere."

"Good, I would hate to see you go. You are my best friend and I love you like a sister!"

"I feel the same. Now go out there and sit would ya?" I say ushering her outside smiling the whole time thanking Mama and Grandpa once again for bringing me to Colvin. To this wonderful life I am beginning to have.

"Mom, I need your help."

"What do you need help with Son? Everything okay?"

"Everything is perfect; I just need to do something for Leah and I can't do it alone."

"What's that?"

"Shannon is buried in New York and when we were there for the trial, she wanted to go see her. We did that but she said she feels guilty for leaving her behind when she moved here."

"Oh that's sad. You should do a memorial site here for her."

"That's exactly what I was thinking. Where do you think I should do it?"

"Is there somewhere she loves the most here?"

"Besides the nursery? Um, well maybe the lookout spot on top the hill."

"You could do it there then. It's got the best view on the property."

"Yes, but what do I do for a marker? Have a large stone carved or what?"

"Well, Aiden had a stone carved for Karlie's dad Gene. Let's call him and see where he got it done at." She dials Aiden's number.

"Hey Son. Austin and I are here trying to figure out a marker for a memorial site we're working on for Leah's daughter Shannon. We were wondering where you got the marker you did for Gene. Oh really? Can you get the number to Austin? Thanks Son. How's Karlie today? Shouldn't be too much longer. Love you two. Bye."

"He says he got it from that stone place on the southeast side of town. They do a lot of the headstones for the cemetery. He said he'll text you the name and number."

"I think that will be the best place to have it. Do you think she will be okay with it Mom?"

"Leah will be so touched Austin. I can make you guys a picnic and you can take the horses out there again, make a day of it."

"Thanks Mom you're the best."

"Here's the number. I'm gonna go call them and head back to town. Leah should be done having lunch with Karlie by now. Love you Mom. Thanks for your help!"

"Anytime Son. If you need more help, just let me know."

******************

Austin has been acting so weird the past couple of days. Seems to have a lot of calls to make which always take him in the next room. Weird.

"Hey babe, what are you doing?"

"Hey Leah, I'm going to go deliver this order and be back later. Love you." And he leaves without even asking me to go with him. That is even weirder. I didn't know anyone even ordered that many pink rose bushes.

I am looking in the files for the ticket for the rose bushes but see nothing. He must have forgotten to write it up or took it with him. I guess we'll see later who needed that many of the rose bushes I like the most.

"Karlie, how are you feeling today?" I ask once she picks up the phone.

"Fat and miserable. This kid is never going to come out. I'm going to be preggo forever."

I laugh and say, "She'll come out any day now. She can't wait to meet her Mommy and Daddy."

"And Aunt Leah!"

"Not Aunt yet, but soon maybe. Hey, do you know what Austin is up to? He has been acting so strange lately."

"Stranger than normal? He's always strange Leah."

"Yes more than normal. He's always going outside to talk on the phone like I'm not supposed to hear and he just left with a large order of rose bushes that I can't find the ticket on."

"He's stealing rose bushes? That is so strange for a nursery owner. You're paranoid Leah."

"Maybe you're right. I'm trying to find something wrong aren't I?"

"Yes, I think you are.  Austin loves you and isn't up to anything. Well, anything illegal anyway ha ha!"

"You are no help Karlie!"

"You called me, remember?  Ok, gotta go pee.  Love you!"

"Love you too."

Ok, she was no help.  Oh well, I better get these invoices entered into the system and get statements out before Austin gets back. Maybe we can close up early and go home.  I want to get through a little bit more of Grandpa and Grandma's stuff in the attic.

## 45

"Hey baby, what's up? What have you found up here this time?"

"Austin, where have you been? I have been trying to get ahold of you for hours! I finally just closed the nursery and came home. Where have you been?"

"I'm sorry; I went out to the 6AB to help with a couple new horses. Didn't I tell you I was doing that after the delivery?" he says and kisses my forehead.

"No, you didn't say a word. I was worried about you. I even called Karlie and she didn't know anything."

"I'm sorry Leah. I should have made sure you knew where I was going. Next time I will make sure you know, okay?"

"Okay, you owe me though."

"Deal." And he moves over next to me and starts sifting through trunks that belonged to my grandparents.

"Wow, look at this picture Leah. Your Grandpa and Grandma look so young."

"Oh my goodness. That was the day they got married. My Dad really looks like Grandpa."

"And you look just like your Grandma."

"You think so?"

"I do. Look at this one. You had to be what? Five?"

"Oh my goodness yes I was five. Austin, you're in this one."

"No... Can't be me."

"It is, look. You and I are actually getting along long enough to get a picture taken together."

"That was after my thirteenth birthday party. I couldn't believe you were there that day."

"Grandpa made me go. That part I remember. I didn't know what to get you or what to say to you so I just sat there alone wishing I could go home."

"It was the best birthday ever because you were there." He wraps his arms around me and kisses the side of my head.

"I was such an ugly little kid."

"You were far from ugly. I had a huge crush on you. Still do actually."

"You were blind. Oh my goodness, look at this one. This must be Mom and Dad's wedding day. I have never seen this one. She looks so gorgeous and Dad looks so happy."

"Your mother was beautiful. I see where you get your beauty."

"Oh please. You are just saying that to get a little."

"No, I'm not just saying that. I wouldn't mind getting a little as you put it, but I really do believe you are beautiful. Even when you wore all that makeup and high dollar clothing I thought you were gorgeous. The first time I saw you again in Roger's office it took all the self-control I had not to reach over and touch that amazing hair of yours. That blue dress you had on was amazing."

"Funny thing is that I wanted so badly to feel these arms and this chest that day. I was practically drooling over the hot cocky cowboy that I met that day. Then to find out you were the same one I liked all those years ago. Who would have guessed we would be so in love now."

"Seems everyone else knew but us. I am not complaining though." He stands us up and wraps me completely in his arms while putting that hot mouth on mine.

Once I moan he knows that's a good sign and starts to move down my neck with those hot kisses that make me feel alive and on fire.

"I'm not sure I can wait until we get to the bedroom Leah."

"Who says we have to wait? There's a blanket over there. You up for making love up here in the attic cowboy?"

"I am up for making love to you anywhere Princess."

## 46

"Now once she gets here, we'll ride up there and after about fifteen minutes you guys can all come and join us. Sound good?" I say to the rest of my family.

"Sounds good Austin. We better all scatter because I think she just came through the main gate."

After everyone disappeared just in time, I see Leah's pickup come into view and head my way. Seeing this woman pull up and smile at me makes my heart leap from my chest. I am so nervous that she won't like this surprise.

"Hey cowboy. What's up? Why did you want me to meet you out here? Are we going for a ride?"

"Whoa girl, one question at a time." I lean down and kiss her lips. She wraps her arms around my neck and kisses me back. Her in my arms is all that matters anymore. I pray she feels the same after our little horseback ride.

"Ready to go for a little ride? I have a surprise for you."

"Really? I'm ready. Do I get a hint?"

"No. You'll have to wait and see."

"After you cowboy."

"Follow me Princess."

After the short ride to the special spot, I turn to her and see she's once again mesmerized by the sites.

"I still can't believe you guys own all of this. It's so beautiful! I could stay up here for hours."

"Well, I'm glad to hear you say that because your surprise is up here." I gesture towards the right of where we are standing. Dismounting and helping her to do the same I see her looking around trying to understand what the surprise is. As she hits the ground though and turns around she sees exactly what she was meant to see.

"Oh my Austin! What have you done?" she yells and runs towards the spot picked out especially for her.

"My family and I have been working on this spot for you and Shannon to be able to be together. We planted all the small pink rose bushes that you like too. Aiden got me in contact with a wonderful stone carver which made the memorial stone for Shannon. You can come here anytime you want to be alone with her now and not feel guilty about being away from New York."

She sits there hunched over crying making me unsure if she's happy or upset.

I walk up towards her saying, "Leah are you upset with me? We all thought you would love this. Were we wrong?"

"Oh my goodness Austin, no you weren't wrong. I am so overwhelmed with emotion right now. I'm not sure what to say. I cannot believe you did something so amazing for me. And for Shannon." She walks to me and lays her head on my chest while wrapping her arms around my waist.

"So you are happy? It's not too much or invasive?"

"Austin it is beyond perfect. It is the most amazing thing anyone has ever done for me. And to think your family helped you do this. It's just so much and I don't know how to ever thank you."

"They'll be along here in a few minutes to make sure you like it. You can tell them then."

"I love it so much and I love you even more Austin. Thank you so much for bringing her and me this special place."

While we stand in front of Shannon's memorial stone and bushes, we can hear my family start to draw near. They opted to drive the pickups instead of riding horses. Karlie is even in the back seat. Should have known she wouldn't miss this moment for her friend.

\*\*\*\*\*\*\*\*\*\*\*\*\*\*\*\*\*\*

"I can't even begin to thank all of you for what you have done here. You have given me a spot where I can come to talk and feel closer to Shannon while I'm away from New York."

"Leah, you are a very important part of our family and we were all very happy to be a part of this special surprise. You deserve the world and we are happy to have been a part of giving you a small special part of it here in Colvin." Amelia comes up to me and hugs me and kisses the side of my head.

"Karlie Mae, you knew about this when I asked you why Austin was being so weird didn't you?"

"Maybe a little bit. There was no way I was giving away the surprise."

"Thank you for not giving it away. Could you take a picture of this so I can frame it to hang in my house? I love it and I love you all so much." I walk from person to person giving them a hug and big thank you.

"After you were so upset to leave Shannon at the cemetery in New York, I got to thinking you needed something here so I called Mom and she's been helping me along with everyone else to get it perfect. Your father helped us to figure out the flowers to use here. He said the small pink roses would mean the most to you. He was upset he couldn't make it today for the reveal but knew you would be surrounded by love." Austin puts an arm around my waist and draws me near to his side.

I look around at the gathering of wonderful people that I now call friends. One day soon I might even call them family. I turn to sit next to the stone with Shannon's name on it and hear everyone start to leave. I kiss my fingers and place them on her name like I always do at her grave in New York. My heart is so full of happiness and love. I have everything I could ever ask for here in Colvin now. Absolutely everything.

## 47

"Austin, is Leah with you?  Please tell me she's with you!  I tried calling her but she didn't answer." I hear Karlie frantically asking me from the other end of the phone line.

"No, I'm at the nursery and she's at home I believe.  Why? What's up?" I wonder why she's so upset.  Maybe she just broke a nail or found a gray hair or something.  I will never understand women.

"I'm at mom's shop and I think she might have done something bad.  Really bad."

"What could your sweet little mama have done that's bad?" I smile visualizing how sweet Ella Mae is and how good she has been to Aiden and our family throughout the years.

"There was a man in the store earlier and you know my mom, she didn't put two and two together when he was asking random questions about Leah.  She just figured he was someone new in town that had been by the nursery and met her.  But Austin, I think he was a reporter.  There are tons of them outside the store now trying to get in but we locked the door. They are trying to get us to tell them where to find Leah. Oh Austin, where is she? We need to warn her and get her out of sight."

I hear her take a deep breath knowing I had trouble following all of that long winded reply. I drop the hammer and run to the front of the nursery locking doors behind me. I have got to get to Leah and take her to the 6AB. No one will be able to bother her there. She is going to be so freaked out.

"I'll go get her and take her to the 6AB. Get your mom out of there and meet us at Mom & Dad's. And be careful. They are like vultures. Try not to let them follow you if you can help it."

"Ok we'll meet you there. Austin we are so sorry! Leah is never going to forgive us for this."

"She'll be ok don't worry. Just get your mom and get out." By now I am flying down the nursery driveway and turning onto the paved city road. Leah only lives a few blocks away from here so it shouldn't take me long to get there.

Oh crap! They are here too! How in the world did they find the house? It's registered to her grandparents so someone did their homework. I pull up into the driveway and into the garage shutting the garage door behind me and stand behind my pickup to make sure no one got in.

Once it shuts, I rush into the house yelling Leah's name. When she doesn't answer me I realize it's because she is clear up in the attic and wouldn't be able to hear me or the paparazzi outside. But when I pass by the bedroom I see that she's curled up with her favorite blanket sound asleep on the bed. She must have worn herself out. I smile and feel a lot better knowing she is oblivious to the circus outside. But instantly frown knowing that I have to be the one to tell her about it.

I lean down and kiss her cheek saying her name lightly. She stirs, smiles and stretches.

"I must have fallen asleep. I didn't mean to actually sleep. I was just exhausted from moving all that stuff around up there and sat down for a second. Well, I guess not a second if it's what? Three o'clock? Oh my goodness I didn't done near what I wanted to today." She stands up and hugs me tightly making my heart melt.

"It's okay Princess, no one will ever know." I smile, wink and kiss her forehead trying to put off telling her something that is sure to spoil her good mood.

"Why are you home so early? I didn't think you would be done with that shed until much later."

"I think you need to look out the window." I point towards the bedroom window that faces the front of the house.

She looks at me strangely but complies then whips back from it as quick as she opened it.

"Oh my gosh Austin, how did they find me?" Tears start to form in her eyes and I see she is shaking.

"Karlie called me and said that Ella Mae might have told one some information about you before she realized who he was. You know how friendly she is. They both feel terrible. I told them to load up and head to the 6AB and we would meet them there. Do you need to change or anything?"

"No, let's go. I don't want to be this close to them any longer than I have to. But how am I going to get out of here without them seeing me?"

"I parked in the garage; you crawl in the back seat and cover up with the blanket. Stay there until we get off the pavement."

"Deal. I just can't believe this is happening. I thought I was safe here."

"You are safe Leah, especially once we get you to the ranch."

"Ok let's go." She wipes the tears away and storms for the stairs.

As we pull out of the garage and then the driveway once the door shut, I see the swarm of photographers rushing around the pickup snapping shots and yelling questions left and right. This is craziness! It's worse than the day at the courthouse in New York. No wonder Leah wanted away from there so badly.

"It's clear Leah. You can climb up here now. No one's following us."

"That you can see." She sits there pouting like a two year old and it makes me chuckle.

"How do you find this even the least bit funny?"

"The situation isn't funny Princess, you sitting there looking like a child is." I smile and pinch her cheek. That makes her pout more but at least she lies over the console onto my shoulder. Any contact with her makes me happy. Even if there is a console in between us, I'll take it.

## 48

Pulling up to ranch house, we see Mom and the whole family come out running. They all swarm around Leah asking if she's ok. I pause and just watch my family clucking around Leah like mother hens. We all thought Mom was the smothering one, well from my view everyone is doing it. It warms me to know that they are as willing to accept and protect Leah as I am. This really is the woman for me.

"Guys, guys. Why don't you let her get inside?" I say pushing others away and wrapping my arm around Leah. Everyone cracks a grin knowing I'm getting territorial.

"Leah dear, are you okay? We have been so worried about you since Karlie and Austin called us." My Mom says as she wraps her arms around the other side of Leah and ushers us inside.

"I'm fine, just a little shaken up. I never dreamed they would come here."

"Well, they won't be coming on this property so you are safe now." I hear my Dad say while holding open the door for the lot of us.

"Thank you AJ, it means the world to me. I'm so sorry this is involving your family."

"You are family now Leah. What happens to you happens to us." Dad puts his finger under her chin and lifts her head to look into his eyes. I see she's crying again but trying to hide it. Dad sees through it and pulls her into his arms. She looks so small there. It breaks my heart to see her so upset.

"Let's get you something to drink dear. Would you like coffee or tea?"

"A strong cup of coffee would be amazing Amelia. Thank you."

"No need to thank me. You heard AJ say you were a part of this family now."

"That means so much to me. More than you all will ever know."

"Now we just need to figure out what they want and how they found you." I say and pull a bar stool out for Leah to sit on.

She nods and sighs bigger than I think she realized she was going to do. She looks at me and tears start to form again. Just as she is going to let loose the back door opens and Karlie flies in screaming Leah's name.

"Oh my goodness Leah we are so, so, so sorry for this! We didn't realize what they were asking all that information for."

"Don't worry about it. They were bound to find me and can be sleazy anyway. Don't beat yourself up about it. You got word to me in time and luckily I wasn't where they could see me anyway."

"I'm afraid we have company outside the gate." We all turn to see Aiden come into the room from the front door.

"They followed Karlie in didn't they? Gosh darn it! Those buggers had better not come on this property or I'll be using them for target practice!" Dad says making us all laugh. Great way to diffuse the tension in the room. I look at Leah and even she was laughing and could see the clouds part in her eyes. Maybe she finally realizes she is safe here.

"I called Gene on my way over and he says it's all over the news in New York about Lewis and his sentence. Everyone is wondering where you are and why you weren't seen at the trial. They are speculating that he killed you too."

"Oh my goodness Austin. This is a mess. You hid me a little too well I guess."

"I guess so Princess. What do you want to do?" As I say that my cell phone rings and I see it's Mike and I hand it to Leah.

"Hi Dad. Yes, they're all over town. Some even made their way to the gates of the 6AB. No, no one has seen me yet. I hid under a blanket when we left my house. I was working in the attic all day so I wasn't out in the open. I know its nuts. They think I'm dead too? Crazy. You are welcome to come spend time here to get away from them. I don't know what to do either Dad. You really think so? You think that would be the best thing? Then they would leave me alone?" We all stare straight at Leah as she talks to her dad. This isn't sounding like something I'm going to be happy about.

"Well, Dad thinks I should call a press conference or do an interview setting the record straight that way they will leave me alone." She looks up at me with questions in her eyes. I can see she's as uncomfortable about that idea as I am.

"That's up to you Princess but I don't like it."

"Your dad's right though. Once you take away the story, they will go away. They won't find the need to hound you anymore. That's what Gene suggested too I just didn't want to tell you yet." Karlie says and takes Leah by both hands standing in front of her.

"You think so? Where would I do it and with whom? What do I say?"

"I have a girlfriend that owns the radio station in town. Maybe that would be the best way to go so that you don't have to do it on camera? Do you think I should call her? Austin you remember Margaret don't you?"

"Mom, that's brilliant. Margaret was the one that let us announce the songs when you would go visit her. We used to be the best DJ's ever."

"Austin, you two were never really on air you know. She made you think that so you would behave. I'll go give her a call."

"That might be just the way to do it Leah. I can't take some pictures for you that we can send along with the transcript of the recorded interview to the big people in New York and get it all over with that way." Karlie says as the whole plan starts to make sense to her. She's jumping up and down now the best she can with the belly she has.

"That sounds like a pretty good plan, doesn't it Princess?" I ask Leah and squeeze her shoulder hoping she will be truthful and not just go along with their plan if she isn't on board.

"That actually sounds like something I am comfortable with. If I have to do it at all, I can handle this. Thank you all so much for your help." She says and hugs everyone until Mom comes back into the room with the news that Margaret will swing by around dinner time.

"You better go call your Dad and let him know the plan. You can use my phone in Dad's den." I hand her the phone and point her to the right room. I feel so much better about this situation now. Mom's awesome.

"That poor girl has been through Hell and back. I sure hope this doesn't get her down." Dad says and walks out the back door. Too much touchy feely for that tough old guy. I smile and sit down on the bar stool Leah vacated.

"Mom, did you bake anything today?" I smile knowing there's a fresh batch of chocolate chip cookies somewhere in this kitchen. Mom always makes cookies when someone is in turmoil.

Once I find the sweet mountain of goodness, I take a few and walk to where Leah is standing deep in thought by the window. As I get closer, I see she's crying.

I wrap my around her from behind and whisper in her ear, "It's gonna be okay Princess. I promise."

"I just can't believe they came here Austin. I really thought I was over all this." I feel her shake a little.

My heart breaks to see her so upset. I wish there was something I could do to help her feel better. But I know there really isn't anything I can do this time. Just being here and loving her is the best I can do.

"I love you Leah. Never forget that. No one will ever hurt you again." I pull her tighter against me and kiss the top of her head.

## 49

"Leah, if you want to just sit here while we get the equipment set up that would be great. It should only take a few more minutes." I hear Margaret say to me through the haze in my head. I can't believe I'm doing this. What was I thinking? I look up to find Austin with his arms across his chest and swaying from side to side with a devilish look on his face. I have a feeling he isn't too happy about this either.

"How much longer does she have to sit there waiting? We need to get this over with." Austin says looking even more annoyed and walks over to the head technician. They continue to have quite the heated encounter resulting in AJ coming to the technician's rescue. I see Austin stalk off towards the outer edge of the group. Poor guy is taking this harder than I am. That helps ease a bit of my tension. I look up and see Amelia looking my way and give me her sweet calming smile. I breathe in deep and let it out slowly. Along with the breath going out of my body I also feel some of the tension and fear goes too.

"Leah, are you ready for this? I will get some shots of you next to Shannon's gravestone if you want me to. You said you wanted to have the interview done here for that reason right?" Karlie says from my left side. She has set up her camera and tripod up on that side because that's where the light was the best.

I wanted to do the interview from Shannon's memorial site because she is as much a part of this as I am. The world will find out about her regardless if I tell the story or not. I never wanted them to know about her but it's time to get it all out so that I can move on this time.

"Ok Leah we're ready to begin the interview. Are you ready?"

"Yes, I'm ready. Thank you again for doing this on such short notice." I look at Austin and smile the best smile I could muster to ease his frustration. He smiles back and mouths "I love you". I can't believe I have been blessed with such a wonderful human being to be in my life.

"Today we have the pleasure of spending some time with Leah Frankle. You all might know her as the wife of New York Yankees pitcher Lewis Frankle. But what you all may not know is that she has not been married to Mr. Frankle for almost a year now. I'll let Leah recount the day things went terribly wrong in the Frankle household resulting in Leah fleeing New York for the small town life in Oklahoma. Leah?"

"Hello, um the night you're talking about started with Lewis having a home game against the Red Sox. He was hurt and unable to pitch that season and wasn't handling it well. He would come home drunk and angry after games that he felt he could have won if he were the one pitching. I was upstairs putting baby clothes away when he came home. As you all know I was pregnant with our first child at the time. But when Lewis came home and became violent with me, I fell down the stairs." I pause and start to feel tears start to burn my eyes. My hands are shaking and my breathing is getting shorter. Losing Shannon is the worst part of this whole story. I'm not sure I can say it. How do I tell the world I lost my little angel that night?

"Leah, you don't have to do this. Come here." I feel Austin pull me up from the chair and into his arms. Once I get into them I lose my composure. Being in his arms is where I feel safest. Where I feel the least judged. I cry my eyes out and start to feel my heart feel less wounded and start to pull away. I look up at him and smile.

"I'm good now. Thank you." He smiles and kisses my forehead. As he walks away I feel a wave come over me like a renewed energy. I think I'm ready to do this. I put my hand on Shannon's headstone and say a quick prayer. I can do this.

"Ok, are you ready to finish Leah? We are close to the end. Let's start with your accident. You said that Lewis was violent and belligerent when he came home. When you went to help him to bed he ended up pushing you down the stairs correct?"

"Yes, I feel down the stairs and landed on the marble tile at the bottom. I don't remember much after that until I woke up in the hospital. And my father had to tell me that I lost my baby. The impact made on the way down the stairs and at the bottom was too much for her to handle." I breathe in deep and try to keep going.

"Leah's housekeeper was the one who found her at the bottom of the stairs and called 911 along with her father. The ambulance came and rushed her to the hospital where Mike Stampley, Leah's father, met them. Once he found out what had happened and that Leah was out of immediate danger, he went to Leah's house looking for Lewis. He did find him there but he had passed out from all the alcohol. Mike sat in the chair next to Lewis' bed awaiting him to wake up from his alcohol induced slumber."

"When Lewis woke up Dad told him what had happened and made a deal with him to give me a quiet divorce and leave me alone for the rest of my life. He went to rehab and I buried my daughter. No one was supposed to know about any of it so that I could pick up the pieces and move on with my life. I moved to Colvin after my Grandfather willed me part ownership in his nursery. It's here that I have found who I used to be and whom it is I'm supposed to be now."

"It was here that you fell in love again too. The other part owner of the nursery is Austin Blake from here in Colvin, Oklahoma. Austin and Leah have known each other since they were children running around the nursery. Austin has worked at the nursery with Leah's grandfather since he was old enough to have a job. He fell in love with Leah when she was a lanky young girl who would come visit her grandparents during the summer."

"Ok Austin, we're ready for you." Austin walks towards me smiling and sits in the chair to my right. I feel his warmth on my legs and make the beat of my heart speed up. My heart swells knowing this is the man I was meant to spend my life with. He grabs my hand and intertwines our fingers. His touch will forever make me tingle.

"We now have Austin Blake joining us here in the memorial site he made for Leah's daughter. Is that correct?"

"Yes ma'am. Leah was very upset that she left her daughter's grave in New York and felt as though she abandoned her. So, I had this spot made for her so that she had one here where she could feel her little girl. My whole family helped get it just right and finished for Leah. We all love her very much." He squeezes my hand and I hear the rest of his family murmur their sentiments making me smile again.

"Thank you all so much for what you did and continue to do for me. This spot where I can come and feel close to my little girl is just perfect. There isn't a day that goes by that I don't miss her but I know that everything happens for a reason. I truly believe that all of this tragedy was meant to bring me here to Colvin to see Austin again. He is my future and being a part of his family means the world to me."

"You look like you have made the best of the tragedy that happened to you Leah. Unfortunately that isn't the end of the story where Lewis is concerned. Lewis was arrested and charged with first degree murder and attempted murder early this year. Leah was subpoenaed and testified for the prosecution where they found him guilty and sentenced to life in prison. While Leah is in this small town trying to heal and move on with her life, she would appreciate the press giving her the privacy she has been seeking. So, now that Leah has told us what really happened we can understand why she disappeared. A big thank you to Leah and Austin for taking time out of their lives to set the record straight and help us all to understand what happened to Leah. We fell in love with Leah in the Chanel ads we saw her in and can now fall in love with the small town girl she has become. Thanks again. Have a good day. I'm Margaret Fallon with CRB Radio from Colvin, Oklahoma."

"Thank you Margaret. You made this easy and made it pleasant. I really appreciate your help. Have a good day."

"Karlie did you get the shots you needed or are we done here?"

"I got them. I will work on them and email them to you late this evening. I'll see you guys later. You both did great!"

"Thanks Karlie. I appreciate the help. Let me know how they turn out." I say and give her a hug as she tries to leave. I'm hoping the pictures turn out good and I don't hate them all. I haven't allowed myself to be photographed since before the accident. I have been too self-conscious about how I look even though all the wounds have healed.

Everyone says their good-byes and I ask Austin to leave me for a few minutes alone with Shannon. He kisses me and leaves with his parents. I walk to her headstone and kneel down laying my head on the cool shaded stone.

"Oh baby girl, what have I gotten myself into? I can't believe I just did that interview. Do you think it will be ok? Austin says it will but I'm not so sure they know what they have gotten into either."

After sitting here for a while I feel a little calmer than I had before. Things might actually work out ok. Once Margaret gets the interview transcribed and sent to the newspapers in New York, I can only pray this nightmare is concluded. I don't know how much else I can handle.

## 50

"Hey Leah, how are you?  What can I get for ya this morning?" Sally says as I walk into the café before going to the nursery this morning.  It has been a couple of days since the interview and sent to New York.  I'm not sure how it's being perceived but hopefully well, I couldn't handle the attention it could bring if it's not good.

After ordering my food, I smile at Sally and turn to walk to a booth.  As I reach the seat I can sense someone standing next to me and I look up to see a gentleman I have never seen before.  He smells of alcohol and cigarettes but his face is calm and smiling.

"Hello, can I help you?"

"Well, I would say you have done enough." He slurs out.

"I'm sorry, do I know you?"

"No, prefer it that way with what you did to that husband and his girlfriend." His face starts to look angry.

"Um, I don't know what you're talking about."

"Oh you know. You come here to get old' Austin to murder the hubby so you can have all his Yankee money but got the girlfriend instead. How did you do it?"

"Excuse me sir, but you have had way too much to drink and don't have a clue what you're talking about."

"Ya right lady. I solved the mystery and know you're toxic and up to no good here. I'm going on out to that 73X ranch or whatever it's called and put a stop to this tragedy."

"Well, you do just that then if you know so much." I am in such shock and angry by this I storm out of the café without getting my order. I can hear Sally yelling after me but I don't stop. I can't stop. How can someone even think that Austin or I would do such a thing?

Walking down the street I can see everyone's heads turn to look at me. They are looking like I'm a menace. All of them have furrowed brows and frowns on their faces. How could this be happening?

As I turn the corner by the grocery store, I see the newsstand with my face plastered all over it. Oh no! When I get close enough, I can see it's one of those trashy gossip magazines that think they know the whole story. Think. Oh my goodness. This is where that guy had to have gotten his story. In a fit of rage I rip the entire supply off of the shelves and pay for each one. Leaving none there for another person to chance upon and draw their conclusions from. As I do, I look around to see everyone in the store frowning at me too. Children are pointing and their parents are shushing them. This is a scene right out of a movie, not my life. How can this be my life?

As I'm rushing out of the store, I about run a poor little old lady over in my haste. There's one more reason to be the outcast.

This feels so strange to me. This morning I was a part of this happy little town and now I'm an outcast and a murderer. How did this happen? How could everyone believe it? What do I do now? I can't live like this again with the world watching every move I make.

Dad. I can go stay with Dad. Austin can handle the nursery. I've got to get away from this. I can transfer my ownership and never have to come back.

Austin. What do I tell him? Do I tell him? No. I can't face him after what that man said, the looks and the magazines.

Reaching my house I run upstairs and call Dad while I pack. He'll understand and think I'm doing the right thing. Good old' Dad.

## 51

"Hey Mike, what's up? How's Martha's Vineyard?" I say answering my cell phone call from Leah's Dad.

"Austin, you really need to go talk to Leah. She just called me in a total panic and said she was packing to leave Colvin for good. She's very upset and talking about transferring you complete ownership and everything. You have to hurry Austin before she does something she's going to regret later."

"Leaving? What's she so upset about Mike? She was fine when I left this morning."

"Have you seen any of the gossip magazines today? I guess she has and they aren't flattering. Some drunken man confronted her at the café. She's supposedly on the cover Austin. You know how that's going to make her feel. She's freaking out."

"Oh no. This was what the interview was supposed to alleviate. I'm at the 6AB right now but I'll head to town. I'll find her Mike, don't worry. No one cares what these magazines have to say. I'll call you once I find her. Thanks for the head's up."

"Take care of her Austin, please. She's very skittish right now. Keep me in the loop. Bye."

I dial Karlie but she doesn't answer. I look at the clock and see that it's probably because she's napping. Crap. I guess it really doesn't matter what the magazines say. I just have to find Leah and pray it's not too late.

*********************

I can't get my pickup to start. "Come on you dumb thing. You are brand new, why won't you start??" Arg! I beat my hands on the steering wheel knowing it is very dire that I get out of this town.

After trying it for several minutes I realize it's no use. I'm stuck here in the garage with the world hating me on the other side. And I bet Dad called Austin and he's on his way. I feel so helpless and embarrassed I can't imagine being face to face with Austin. If this stupid pickup would just start! How can it not start? I'm taking you back to the dealership tomorrow and trading you off!! Grrrrr!

Bawling my eyes out and trying not to pass out, I try the ignition one more time knowing I'm only dreaming. It fires!! Yes, I can leave now! I open the garage door and ease out onto the driveway and when I turn to hit the button to make the garage door shut, I realize this might be the last time I see this house. I really don't think I will ever be welcome here in Colvin again. I sigh and raise my eyes to the rear view mirror and ease off the brakes again.

But, I freeze because who do you think has pulled up right behind me? Austin. I see him throw the door open and come running to my driver's door. The door won't open because it's locked and he just stands there frowning at me. Dad did call him and of course he dropped everything to come talk me out of leaving. I can't look at him though. I don't want him here; I just want to leave Colvin and all this behind.

"Leah roll down the window!" he looks angry now. Oh boy. I can't just back out and drive away either. His pickup is keeping me here and I'm sure that's how he planned it. I touch the switch and roll the window down but refuse to look at him.

"Leah where are you going Princess?" I see him look in the seat next to me at my suitcase. Yep, Dad talked to him alright. Why did you have to call him? Of all the times not to listen to me....

"Dad's for a while. I need to get on the road though, my flight leaves in a few hours. Please move your pickup." And I roll the window back up leaving him standing there stunned and angry.

"Why are you leaving so sudden? You didn't say a word about that this morning when I left. What happened?"

"I don't want to talk about it Austin. Just let me go. Please."

He walks over to the passenger side of the pickup and opens the door. Why did I put it in park? I didn't think about it unlocking once I did that. Grr! Once he opens the door all the way he sees the gossip magazine on the floor board. Oh great. He looks through it and frowns when he sees the picture of walking into the courthouse in New York. There are some of us at Lewis' trial, at the cemetery, and even holding hands in Sally's. I feel so ashamed now that I see him seeing this in the magazine. He has to hate me. This is the reason I didn't want or need a man in my life.

"Is this what has you so spooked? Why you're running away from me now too?"

"Austin, please don't. I can't do this again." I look at him and my heart melts when he smiles. Smiles? How can he be smiling in the middle of this mess?

"Don't what? Don't love you? I'm sorry to tell you Princess but I love you way too much to just let you drive out of my life like this. If you leave, I'm going with you. We a nursery full of flowers that won't make it a day or two without water but I'm ok with that if you are. I thought the pictures were good, we could put them in a scrapbook." He smiles that evil little smile and his eyes are sparkling. How can he think this is a joke?

"Austin, seriously. This is horrible. You can't leave but I need to. You have your whole family and your whole life here. This is where you belong."

"You are my life Leah. Wherever you are is where I belong. Why can't you get that through your pretty little head?" I just notice that he's sitting in the passenger seat now. How sneaky, I didn't even realize until now.

"Your family is such a big part of this town and all this negative press isn't good for them. The nursery is going to be taking a hit too once every one hears it. You should have seen the way everyone was looking at me when I left Sally's. Some guy chewed me out there right next to a booth so I left without even getting my food. Austin I was so embarrassed and upset. I can't do this again!" I start to tear up again but swallow down the mass of emotion threatening to escape.

"Leah, if you're talking about George the town drunk, then you should know he's just talking out of his butt. He probably saw the article while he was waiting in line for another bottle of whiskey. He's not someone you should be basing all of this on. He once chewed Audrey out for being so tall. He didn't think women should be so tall. Which meant just taller than him."

I crinkle my eyebrows at him and cock my head. "Before you say another word, no one else has an issue here. Everyone knows the truth and don't believe the articles. Leah, they love you here. You are a part of me, my family and now this town. Why can't you believe that?"

"Austin, you should have seen the way they were all watching me and starting."

"Princess, I'm sure it was just concern. I'm sure they were afraid to see how you would react when you saw the article. Mary that owns the grocery store didn't realize one of the high school kids had put the magazines out. She didn't want them put out. They were supposed to be sent back. Every other store in town has done the same."

You really think that's what it was? Austin, I don't want to make anyone uncomfortable. It's the last thing I want to do. You aren't mad that you were dragged into a murder plot story?"

He chuckles and says, "Mad? Not in the least. I think it's kinda funny. Like we could ever do anything like that. And when would we have had time? The nursery is keeping us both there ten hours a day. It's so farfetched it's hilarious."

"Really? No one hates me? Your family must want to be rid of me though."

"My family is on their way here right now to try and convince you to stay. I told you we all love you Princess. Especially me. This place would be empty without you Leah. Wanna stay yet?"

"I want to stay yes, I just don't want to cause anyone extra anxiety because of the stories."

"Princess, we are all grownups that can make up our own minds. We know the truth. You are safe here. I promise. Margaret said they have gotten a lot of fan mail you might want to read too."

"Fan mail?"

"Yes, once your story hit, there are a lot of people that felt you were their hero Leah. We can run by and get it from the station if you want to read it. I think it might help you."

"Ok, I think I would like that. I'm curious now to read what they said. Let me pull back into the garage and we can go."

## 52

That was a lot tougher than I thought it was going to be. I honestly thought I would just show up and she would change her mind. It was a little touch and go there for a while. Whew!

"Ready? Let's go." I back out of her driveway and head towards the radio station. I pray these letters help her to feel better. If not, I am at a loss.

We walk inside the door and the receptionist recognizes us at first glance. She calls back to Margaret and she comes up the hallway shortly after.

"Austin, Leah, please come on back. It's so good to see you two again. How's it going?"

"Well, that's why we're here. She saw one of the magazines this morning. Kinda shook her up. I told her you had all that mail for her so she wanted to see it."

"I hope you don't mind that I want to read it all. If it's not for me to see please say. I don't want to intrude."

"Leah, this mail is all addressed to you. Didn't Austin tell you? It's your fan mail. They didn't know where else to send it so it came here. It's all yours." And she picks up a large box and sits it on the floor in front of Leah.

"Oh my goodness, this is all for me?"

"Princess, I told you there was a lot."

"Leah, this is only one of the five boxes. Your story had touched so many women across the country."

"How did me being a coward touch other women? I don't understand."

"YOU are far from a coward Leah. You are a survivor. You did what every abused woman dreams she can do. You got out, picked up the pieces and moved on with your life. You are an inspiration to so many."

"Princess, you are a hero to half the population."

"Wow." Leah looks so overwhelmed. I wrap my arm around her to try and steady her. This is a lot and I'm not sure she has gotten the full impact yet.

"Please, take this box home with you and start reading. Let me know if you want the other four boxes. We get at least fifty pieces every day in the mail. This could be big Leah." She reaches out and touches Leah's arm and I see Leah start to tear up.

"Ok let's get this stuff to your house. You can read some of it and rest. It's been a long morning. Thank you so much Margaret. We'll be in touch."

"Thank you Margaret. I appreciate all you have done."

"Thank you guys. You have done an amazing thing and I see much more in the future. When you're ready there are a few things I would like to run by you. Just take your time and I'll be here when you're ready. Take care."

"See you later Margaret."

"Say hello to your mom Austin."

"Will do thanks." I pick up the box full of sentiments for Leah and lead the way to the pickup. I look back to make sure she is following to find she is smiling. Leah is actually smiling after all this morning brought her way.  Thank goodness.  I can breathe a little easier now.

"Ready to go home?"

"Yes."  She simply smiles and gets into the pickup.  She looks a lot lighter and happier than she did on the way here.

## 53

"Austin, there are letters from women who have lived in abusive relationships for years. Years Austin. Oh my goodness. This lady has lost three babies from the abuse. Oh my goodness is all I can say."

"There are a lot of sick people out there. It's so sad." He sits beside me on the couch and wraps his arm around me slowly pulling me closer. "I am just so thankful you made your way to me."

"Me too Austin. I didn't have it as bad as most of these women do. He only got violent after a game and I usually tried to steer clear of him when that happened." I shiver at the memories. Even this long after it still makes me shiver knowing how scary things were and how much worse they could have been.

"You should start a charity for abused women Leah. You would be amazing at that."

"What do you mean a charity? What would I do?"

"It doesn't have to be a charity per say. Could be a cause. You could rally to raise money for abused women and help them get out. That type of thing."

"Austin that's a great idea! I know a lot of people in New York that would help with this type of a cause too. I have to go call my Dad." I smile and run away to call Dad.

"Hey Dad, I think I'm going to start a charity or something that I can help abused women to move on with their lives. What do you think? Yes, I thought so too. He's amazing. Thank you for calling him, I was a little mad at first, but now I'm not. Yes, I would like to stay but I really want to work on this cause. How do I get started? Ok thanks let me know what he says. Love you."

I run back into the living room where Austin is sitting in the same spot reading a letter that was in the box. He doesn't hear me come back into the room but I walk up behind him and wrap my arms around his neck.

"I love you so much Austin. Thank you for fighting to keep me here. I would have regretting leaving you so much. You're my life too." I kiss his cheek and feel him smile. He grabs my arms and swings me over the back of the couch until I'm lying on the couch on my back. I scream and he smiles that heart melting smile.

"I love you too Leah and I'm going to show you just how much." He covers me on the couch and kisses me with so much emotion that I just melt. I love his man and finally have the happily ever after every girl dreams of.

## 54

"Ladies, thank you for coming. I am very excited about this."

"We are just as excited Margaret. Thank you for seeing us on such short notice." Amelia says and sits down in front of Margaret's desk. Audrey, Karlie and I follow sitting down also.

"Leah, this is one thing I had hoped to talk to you about the other day when you and Austin came by. There is such a need for positive influences for women that I am so happy to be able to tell you we are fully ready to back your cause also. We have affiliates all over the country that are also on board. We have helped to raise over $3.5 million dollars so far. Your willingness to tell your story and come forward to give hope to women living in abusive relationships has only added to the allure of this whole cause."

"Wow, I had no idea things could escalate this quickly. Austin and I barely started talking about this a couple days ago." I cover my mouth with my hand and shake my head in shock.

"Leah, the world needs you and your courage. You are the most courageous woman I have ever met. The entire Blake family will be standing right here beside you as you take this new journey. This book you write will help encourage so many women. All the helplines and shelters you help to open will make so many differences for so many women across the country."

"She's right Leah, we have assembled the best team across the country to get this all started. We know you have a lot on your plate with the nursery so we will only need you to be an advocate and involved as much as you would like to be."

"I want to help as much as I can, from Colvin. I can where I'm needed to speak but I don't want to do a book tour unless I have to. I don't want to make any money from this book either. All the proceeds need to go to this cause."

"That can be arranged. Have you thought of a name for this whole cause?" She looks at all of us but lingers on me.

"We have come up with a couple different names but I like one in particular. Austin and I agree that it should be called "Shannon's Crusade". The homes we open for the women I would like to be called "Shannon's Home". What do you all think?" With that I shake and start to tear up knowing how many little Shannon's weren't able to live a life because of the abuse.

"Oh Leah that's perfect! There couldn't be a more perfect name!!" Amelia hugs me from the side and I see she has teared up also. I look at Karlie and she's got tears running down her cheeks like a faucet.

"Karlie, you don't have to cry that hard." I say with a big smile knowing it's more the hormones making her so emotional.

"Shut up Leah you know I love this whole idea so much! And these hormones are killing me!" We all laugh knowing she's a mess.

"You only have a few days left right?" Margaret asked Karlie.

"God willing." And we all laugh again. Poor Karlie, she's so big and miserable. That baby couldn't come soon enough for all of us.

"Leah, we will be in touch. Just start working on the book and we'll get the other balls rolling too. Thank you again. You're such a wonderful woman and I'm very proud to be working with you." She walks around her desk and hugs me tightly. From over her shoulder I see Amelia's face and it hits me hard in the stomach as I see the pride on her face. I pray that's the look my own mother would have on her face if she were here.

"See you later friend. Thank you for all your help." Amelia then hugs Margaret and the rest of us start to head out the door. We all feel so happy and hopeful.

"I guess I have a book to write. See you all later. Thanks again for your support and help. Couldn't do it without any of you." I smile and walk to my pickup. Happy and hopeful myself.

## 55

"Hey Princess. You still writing? It's after midnight. Why don't you come to bed?" I say from the doorway of the living room. I can see her sitting on the couch with her feet propped up on the coffee table. She has her laptop on her lap with fingers going a hundred miles an hour typing.

She stops and looks up at me smiling. "I have almost twelve thousand words already Austin! This is so therapeutic too. I can't seem to get my mind to stop talking and my hands just keep typing what its saying. Should be done in no time."

"Princess you don't have to write a whole book in one night. No one expects that." I walk over and try to take the laptop from her but she frowns at me. I get the hint and sit down next to her instead.

"I just can't stop Austin. It's flowing at such a rapid rate and I'm afraid if I stop my ideas and courage will stop too." She goes back to typing a mile a minute. I shake my head and lay my head on the arm of the couch. Sounds like I'm here for the duration too.

"Ok I'll be right here sleeping. Let me know when you're ready for bed." I close my eyes and the only sound I hear are her fingers on the keys. Crazy woman thinks she has to do it all in one sitting. But there's no changing her mind.

"You don't have to stay down here, go back to the bed where it's more comfortable for you to sleep."

"If you're gonna be down here, then so am I." And with that I don't remember anything else.

\*\*\*\*\*\*\*\*\*\*\*\*\*\*\*\*\*\*\*\*

"Austin, wake up." I whisper in his ear. Poor guy stayed on the couch all night with me. His back and neck are going to be sore today.

"Huh? What time is it?" He looks around for the clock.

"After seven in the morning. You slept on the couch all night. I just finished the book. Well most of it anyway, it's the rough draft. Margaret is going to get me in touch with a publisher today so I can get it sent off and see what they think. I'm sure there will be plenty of changes, but at least the ball is rolling." I hand him a cup of coffee and kiss him lightly on the forehead.

"I can't believe you wrote all night long. And finished it?"

"Well, started it. I will need to explain in more detail in some places I'm sure but they get the gist of it. Is your neck sore? Your back?"

"My neck is yes, but I'll be ok. Wanna shower with me? I know it will feel better then." He wiggles his eyes at me and smiles.

"Sorry but I have to get the nursery opened. I let you sleep longer than I should have. We do have a business to run dear."

"You are pushy woman!" He stands up and slaps me on the bottom making me scream out.

"Hey!" I smile and shake my head.

"You deserved that for making me sleep on the couch." And he disappears upstairs and I head out the door to the nursery. I have work to do and for once I feel as if I can conquer anything that comes my way.

## 56

A few days later we're inside the nursery unloading a bunch of the little pink rose bushes that I always liked. Austin unloads them from the truck and I prune them and set them on the shelves. The last one I take out of his hands has something hanging on one of the branches. I see Austin smile at me once I see it. I reach for the sparkly thing and once I touch it I gasp. Austin stops what he is doing and gets it off the branch for me. I put my hands on my face to cover the shock and emotion that's surely visible.

"Leah, will you be the best part of my day every day for the rest of my life? This life was nothing compared to the way it is now that I have you in it. I would like nothing more than for you to be my wife. To live the life that everyone including your Grandpa envisioned us to have. I love you Leah."

"Oh my goodness Austin. I never expected this. Austin are you sure about this? What if I can't do this again? What if we can't do it? What if something bad happens to us?"

"Leah, baby, take a breath. It's okay. Nothing is going to happen. Our love is stronger than anything out there that could break us apart. I promise to love and take care of you for the rest of our lives. I promise you Leah. What do you say?"

"Yes! I say yes Austin. I love you so much and I can't imagine life without you."

I feel him slip the ring on my finger and I can't help but smile at the simple rose gold band with an oval shaped diamond. Looking closer at it you can see the vines growing up to meet the diamond. How fitting. Austin thought of everything. It's perfect for me.

*******************

"So, what's new with you Leah? Anything at all?" Karlie says across the table from me at Sally's the next day.

"Um, not really. A date was set for a benefit gala in New York for Shannon's Crusade. We got some new cactus shipments today. Maybe you could keep one of them alive." I smile over at her knowing she's talking about the rock on my left hand.

"Leah you are killing me!" She squeals and grabs my left hand holding it up so she can see the ring better. A huge smile never leaving her face.

"Oh that? It's just an engagement ring from the hottest cowboy nursery owner in town!" I try to say calmly knowing I'm dying inside too!

"Leah! When did he ask you? I knew he was thinking about it and trying to find the right time!! Oh my goodness I am so so so beyond happy for you two!!!!"

"Actually he asked me yesterday. We were unloading a shipment and one that he handed me had this ring on one of the branches. It was so romantic Karlie!! I love him so much and can't believe how good he is to me!"

"Ah! I am so excited for you! He's one of the last good ones left. You couldn't have asked for a more perfect man. Well, except for his brother, but I happen to know he's married." She smiles and looks dreamily in love too.

"Who would have thought three years ago we would be married to brothers and living in the same small town in Oklahoma!!"

"I know and I'm so happy you're here!! And of course going to be my sister!!"

"I've never had siblings but I think I hit the jackpot with this family! You are the best a girl could ask for!!"

"We feel the same about you! We all love you so much! Especially me!! And well maybe Austin."

"I think he's a little smitten. I know I am. I LOVE LOVE LOVE this ring!!!"

"Are you ready to go find our handsome men? I miss mine a little too much."

"Here before long you will have to share him you know?"

"Yes and I'm not looking forward to that part!" She laughs and we leave a tip on the table and walk to our cars.

"I'll see you later Karlie. Take care. I'll keep my phone on every night until I know that baby's on its way! Call me, day or night! You hear me?"

"Yes ma'am!"

As I watch Karlie waddle back to her car, I feel my heart swell with more love as I anticipate the joy that baby is going to bring to the Blake family. They are all going to rally around the baby and shower it with more love than you could imagine. That makes me smile knowing that one day I might have a baby for them to shower with love. One day.

## 57

"When's your Dad getting here?"

"Um, I think around four. Why?"

"My parents wanted to have a BBQ tonight for us. For the engagement." The smile on his face never gets old.

"Oh I should have known. An excuse for another family gathering at the 6AB." I say smiling knowing that sounded like a great idea to me too. I love spending time out there and with all of Austin's family. And now I get to introduce my Dad to them.

"You go on out. Dad and I will meet you there once he gets in."

"Okay sounds good. I love you." He kisses me and leaves me breathless like every time he kisses me. This man knows what he's doing.

"Love you too."

After he's gone I shower and get my hair and stuff ready for the evening. We played in the mud a little too much this afternoon and my nails are filthy.  Good thing Karlie and Audrey left their nail kits behind from our last girl's night.

Sitting on the porch doing my nails, I keep stopping to admire the ring on my left hand.  The color of the gold and the shape of the diamond work so well together.  It just doesn't seem real sometimes that I can be this happy.  When I called Dad and told him he was over the moon.  He of course told me that he knew we would end up together.  Just like everyone else seemed to know.  I smile and continue on with my nails.  The worst part of owning a nursery is playing in the dirt and ruining my nails.  Even with dirt all over it, the ring still shines as bright as our future is going to be.

"Hi Dad, how are you?  How was the flight?"  I say running to his open arms as he gets out of the rental car.

"Oh Flower it was a good flight.  I am so glad to be back here with you!  How's the book coming?  Heard from the publisher yet?  Where's that future son in law of mine?" he says smiling from ear to ear.

"He's at the 6AB.  They're hosting a BBQ for us tonight.  They're all waiting.  You need to get spiffed up or are you ready to go? The book is done and in the publisher's hands, but no word yet. Margaret says it could take a while but not to worry. Any more questions?"

"No, but I might change my clothes and wash up a little. I'll be ready in ten."

"Okay I'll see you in ten minutes then. So glad you're here Dad."

"Wouldn't want to be anywhere else Flower." He winks and walks up the stairs to the spare bedroom.

*******************

"Wow I never knew they had such a big ranch. This is all theirs?"

"Yes, it's crazy isn't it? You would expect it to be an old log cabin or some dirty dusty house but it's far from that. You just wait."

"Bigger than the apartment you had on the Upper East Side?"

"Much bigger. And so modern too. I expected this outdated and ugly thing."

"Set your expectations low so you aren't disappointed. Just how I taught ya!" He says sarcastically and we both laugh.

"Oh Dad! Be nice or I'll drop you off here and make you walk the rest of the way."

"Very funny young lady. You wouldn't do that to a poor old man now would you?"

"Try me!" I smile and continue on down the long driveway to the 6AB ranch house where I know there are a whole slew of people waiting patiently for our arrival. Ok, maybe not so patiently if I know Austin at all.

"Holy cow you weren't kidding! It's the biggest house I have ever seen and I have seen big. What a spread they have here. How many acres do they own?"

"I think Austin said like 500. I'm not sure."

"Do we have to take off our shoes and not touch anything inside?"

"Dad! You're doing it again."

"Sorry. I can't help it. Will I ever get used to it?"

"That I can't help with because it's still pretty wild for me too."

I park the car and we start up the sidewalk when the front door opens and out comes Amelia with her kitchen apron on and a very big smile. She must not have been one of the ones waiting patiently either. This makes me laugh and we receive Amelia sized hugs before finally being able to go in the front door.

Once inside the front door though, the rest of the Blake clan hits. Everyone that I know to be a part of this family is here. Of course they are.

"Get used to it Flower, you'll soon be a part of this large group too." I hear Dad say beside me. He must have noticed my pause as I walked into the crowded room. I just smile back at him fully aware of what I'm getting myself into.

"Mike, so glad you could make it!" Austin says and shakes Dad's hand. It makes me smile to see the two most important men in my life getting along.

"I wouldn't have missed it for the world! It's not every day I get invited to a Blake family get together. Nice little spread you have here."

"Thank you. We are very proud of it and proud to have Leah joining our family."

"Thank you AJ, I am also proud to have Austin as my son in law. He is a wonderful man. You have done a great job with him. All of your boys are well mannered gentlemen. You should be proud."

"We are. Would you like something to drink?" Amelia says when she emerges from out of the blue. She smiles knowing she startled all of us.

"Iced tea. You Dad?"

"Iced tea also, thank you." Dad says and puts his arm around my shoulders. He is making sure they know that I am his child and he is only loaning me to them. How funny. Dad is getting territorial.

"Would you like some help in the kitchen Amelia?"

"That would be great, thank you." And with that she and I head to the kitchen leaving my Dad to fend for himself. He's a grown man I'm sure he can handle it. I smile knowing that they will be all chummy before the night's over with.

* * * * * * * * * * * * * * * * * * *

"Mike, this is my older brother Aaron and my little brother Aiden. This is Leah's Dad Mike. He got in just a little while ago from New York. It's so good to have you here with us tonight."

"Austin, it was great to be invited. Anything to see the smile on my baby girl's face. You are good for her. Very good for her. There was a time when I wasn't sure if I would ever see her genuinely happy again. That has a lot to do with you. So thank you." Mike extends is hand again to me and I meet him in the middle but pull him in for a hug. That's what I would do with my own father, why not my soon to be father in law?

"I just annoyed her until she gave into my charms." I smile and chuckle knowing how much we didn't like each other in the beginning.

"Yes, I remember your bickering. Glad to know you're past that. She hasn't looked this happy in a very very long time."

"We are happy. How long are you going to be around?"

"Just the weekend. Gotta get back. I'm doing a little renovating to the new house and the workers will be there Monday morning bright and early. You'll have to visit once they're all done."

"We would love to. Once our niece has made her debut into the world and we're done spoiling her, we just might have to make our way up there. I know Leah really misses having you around."

"I do miss having her around but it's so much easier knowing she has you and your family here to keep her safe and happy."

## 58

"The BBQ was great tonight don't ya think? It was great having your Dad here too."

"Yes, it was great. It was good to see him fitting in with the others so well. I just wish we could get him to move here. It would be even better having him here full time."

"Maybe but he loves Martha's Vineyard and never has liked living here in Colvin."

"I know but it would be great to see him anytime I want. You guys could do all those manly things together too." She smiles and starts to undress. "Can we stop talking about my Dad now?"

"Princess that would be my pleasure." I walk towards her and unbutton my pants and pull my shirt off over my head. She has stripped out of her skirt and shirt leaving her standing there with nothing but a bra, panties and cowboy boots on. She is the sight of an angel with her hair falling down over her shoulders. I suck in a breath and wonder how I am ever going to get used to having such a beautiful creature in my life.

"You are a sight Princess. Come here so I can touch you." She walks to me and just as I reach over to touch her shoulders my cell phone starts to ring on the dresser across the room.

"You better get that."

"No, I'm busy. I can't think I'm going to burst into flames if I can't make love to you." I touch her shoulders and slide my hands up to cup her face. I touch my lips to hers lightly trying to convey just how much I feel for her. She sighs into my kiss and it gets even more heated in the room.

"I want you so badly Austin." She puts her hands on my chest and slides them around my waist. Her touch on me makes me shiver and I take the kiss deeper.

Then her cell phone rings. And she pulls away.

"This could be Karlie or Aiden. Let me get it real quick and then we'll shut them off." She walks to the bedside table her phone is sitting on and answers.

"Hello? Aiden what's up?" She looks over at me knowing we had a lot going on when he called.

"Karlie is in labor. We're on the way to the hospital now. Can you guys come now or did I interrupt something?" He says with so much happiness in his voice.

"We will be right there too! See you there. Tell her we are thinking of her and will pray for her and the baby! Good luck Aiden. Drive safe!" She swirls around with the biggest smile on her face and runs to my arms.

"Karlie's in labor!!! We have to go Austin!!" She kisses my lips so quickly that I would have missed it if I hadn't have been so in tuned with her.

"Ok, get dressed. Let's go. I'll be downstairs waiting."

*******************

"Leah if you don't hurry we're going to miss the birth…." Austin yells from downstairs.

"I'm coming!!" I yell as I start down the stairs. "We don't want to miss your first niece making her way into the world!"

He catches me as I hit the bottom and says with his hands on either side of my face, "OUR niece Leah." I just smile and kiss his lips. I am so excited to meet her!

"I wonder what she'll look like. Whether she'll look like Karlie or Aiden." I say as I look out the window at the Oklahoma sunset slipping below the ground. "I can't wait to be an Aunt!"

"You are going to be a great Aunt! Aunt Leah and Uncle Austin. Hard to believe!!" He says with the biggest smile on his face. His eyes sparkle and I can see the love in them. I envision the joy he will have when our own children are born. I get butterflies in my stomach thinking about that.

******************

"It's a girl! You have a niece!!" yells Amelia so excited! "I have a granddaughter!"

"What did you name her?" I ask Karlie as we step inside her room to see the new family.

"We named her Aleah Mae Blake!" Karlie says smiling and fighting back tears as she watches her daughter be handed between all of her family members. "We named her after you Leah."

I rush to wrap my arms around my friend that has become a sister. "Oh you shouldn't have but I am so honored!!" I am so overcome with emotion and pride that I can't help the tears slipping down my cheeks.

"Will you two be her godparents?" Aiden asks looking at Austin and then to myself.

"Of course we would!" Austin says slapping Aiden on the back and taking his turn holding his new niece. "Look at you beautiful! She looks just like her mommy!"

"She is beautiful isn't she?" I ask him as I stand beside the man I love holding such a beautiful little life. "Are you ready for one of your own?"

"Leah are you serious? You are ready for that?" he says handing off Aleah to his mother and taking me in his arms. "You sure about that?"

"More than anything Austin. But we have to get married first!" I say wrapping my arms around his waist and raising my head to kiss him.

"Today too soon?" Austin asks with a laugh.

"We will start planning when Karlie gets Aleah home. You know she will want to help!" Amelia says coming up and hugging us both. "We can't wait to have you as a part of the family officially Leah."

"Thank you Amelia! I can't wait to be either!" I say smiling and feeling my heart burst with emotions that I have held deep for so long. "It's about time for my happily ever after don't ya think?"

"Absolutely!!" says Karlie loudly before anyone else could respond. Her outburst makes everyone laugh and speak their own agreements.

"Well it's settled then. Leah and I are getting married as soon as you get home Karlie. Are you ready to go now? I can carry the baby." Austin smiles and reaches for Aleah again.

"Austin! Karlie just had a baby you moron. It will be at least tomorrow before she's able to go home. You can hold your horses at least another day or so!" Aiden spits out with a lot of annoyance. He's the protective dad and husband he was meant to be.

I take Austin's hand and kiss the palm. Looking up at him I say, "We can wait another couple of days Aiden. You take care of Karlie and Aleah."

Austin smiles at me and kisses my forehead. "I guess if I have to wait I can. I was only kidding brother. Goodness. I'm not that heartless."

"You'll get your happily ever after, just be patient while mine is recovering from childbirth!" Aiden says and everyone smiles and laughs in unison.

"Boys that's enough, let's let Karlie and Aiden rest. We will see you tomorrow when you get home. Audrey are you ready to go? Where is Audrey? Where did she run off to?" Amelia says looking around the room and out the door. Where could Audrey have gone off to?

# Epilogue

I can't wait to meet my niece. This hasn't been just a long nine months for Karlie and Aiden, but for the rest of us too. I have sat back and watched two of my older brother find their soul mates and now Aiden has his first child too.

It makes me wonder if I will ever find my own happily ever after with a husband and children. I would like nothing more than that but I haven't been lucky enough to find him yet.

I see everyone passing little Aleah around and smiling. They are all so much in love with her after only meeting her minutes ago. We all are so in love with her. My heart leaped so far out of my chest when I saw her sweet little face. That little round button nose just like Karlie's. Seeing my big and strong older brother holding such a little person in his arms was intoxicating. I long to see my husband and child like that. Holding her close in my arms was the greatest feeling I have ever felt before. It made my biological clock start ticking so loud I was afraid the whole world was going to hear it.

My parents are over the moon about becoming grandparents tonight. They will be amazing ones too because they were and continue to be amazing parents. I wonder if Austin and Leah will be next to give them another grandchild?

The little green monster takes a little bit of a hold on my heart as I think of someone other than me being the next one to have a baby. I never realized I wanted one so badly until I say Aleah.

Seeing everyone so happy and fawning over the baby I slip out of the room unnoticed and wander down the hall. I come to the nursery where I can see baby after baby laying in their little clear cribs sleeping. They are sleeping so peacefully while their parents are able to rest a bit before taking them to their new homes.

There's a little boy in the back row that is not happy at all. He's crying and crying wanting someone to pick him up. I can only imagine how upset his mother would be if she knew he was crying so loudly. I don't see a nurse in there with him either. Why isn't anyone helping him?

I see a nurse down the hall so I go to her and ask, "Ma'am there's a little boy in the nursery that is just crying and crying. Why isn't anyone helping him?"

"His mother had a really hard delivery and is resting. There should be a nurse going in soon to help ease him back to sleep. It's ok, thanks for the concern though."

"Oh thank you. It just broke my heart to see him so upset and alone."

She smiles and walks away. I turn and go back to the window of the nursery and see that he has been picked up and now getting a bottle in the rocking chair on the far side of the room. That eases my own anxiety seeing him content and taken care of. Poor little guy. Poor mommy too.

*******************

Sighing I lead my head against the glass and feel the presence of another person next to me. I look over and it's the most handsome man I have ever seen. Sort of tall, dark hair and the most gorgeous brown eyes I have ever seen.

I must be staring because he smiles and asks looking into the nursery, "Which one is yours?"

I look at him for a split second longer and wait for my brain to start working again. Once I realize what he has said I turn back to the window and answer, "None. I don't have any children. Any of them yours?" I secretly hope he says no. I don't see a ring on his left hand so I pray I'm right about him.

"No, none for me either. What are you doing here then?"

"My niece was just born about an hour ago. She's not in here yet though. What about you?"

"Well congratulations Auntie. How exciting."

"Yes, she is just beautiful and our family couldn't be happier to have her here finally. Been a long nine months for all of us."

"I bet. Why don't you have any of your own? Your face lights up when you look at them."

"Ah, well I tend to lean on the traditional side and haven't found the husband yet. What about you?"

He laughs and says, "Same here. I am back and forth from Nebraska and Tulsa that I really don't have time to look. Haven't found Mrs. Right yet either."

"Why are you back and forth so much? Sorry if you don't mind me asking. If it's not too personal for a casual conversation." I redden a bit knowing I'm asking too much.

"It's ok I don't mind. My Mom is here and has been for the past year. She's in the nursing home portion of the hospital for Dementia and Alzheimer patients. She's got Dementia."

"I am so sorry to hear that. That's terrible." I reach out and put my hand on his forearm. Both of us feel the electricity spark between the two of us as I do. He looks down at my hand and I pull it back immediately. "I'm sorry I shouldn't have touched you. I just feel so badly for you."

"Please don't apologize. Not many people know about my Mom and it's nice to talk to someone who cares. Thank you." He smiles and touches my shoulder.

"Why haven't you told anyone?" Ok Audrey you are really getting personal here. You need to just say goodbye and walk away.

"Goodness I can't seem to keep my mouth shut and questions to myself."

"Would you like to go to the cafeteria and get some coffee? I would really like to carry this conversation on a bit longer. I like you a lot. What did you say your name was?"

"Audrey Blake. You really don't have to tell me anymore. I can go so that you can visit with your mother. She must wonder where you are." I turn and start to walk away when he grabs my arm and pulls me back towards him. I feel heat from his skin on my skin and it shocks me.

I look up into his face and he says, "I'm Maysen Correli. Very nice to meet you." He sticks his arm out and initiates a hand shake. I reach out and put my hand in his feeling my skin tingle with awareness as I do. He smiles and turns with my hand still in his and walks us towards the cafeteria. I pull my hand away and follow him. I think at this point I would follow this man anywhere he wanted to go.